Hi, I'm Socially Awkward

Rebekah Brown

To Veronica, who knows what it's like to have an awkward younger sister.

Some lives are changed by a friend or a school dance. Other lives are changed by things, simple objects that for some reason are destined to alter the direction of a life.

An embroidered jacket.

A churro.

An algebra problem.

Too-short gym shorts.

A poorly timed text message.

My life was changed by none of these. Or maybe it was. But I know one thing changed it all.

A jelly bean.

CHAPTER ONE – TUESDAY

Am I weird?

Yes.

Yes, I am.

To be honest, my sister would politely say that I was unique and I would grow out of it. My close friends would say I was "adorably socially awkward" when I interrupted them. And everyone else … well, they said a lot of things that I tried to ignore.

My day began with a buzz breaking the silence of the room. I shifted in bed, blinking in the dark area. Threads of sunlight pierced the cool shade inside, accompanied by a pool of light plastered on the surface of my phone.

I glanced over at it, reading the small letters displayed on the screen.

Brit:
oh my goshhh

Perry:
What is it this time?

Brit:
we have a test today!!!!

Perry:
No, we down.

*don't

Brit:
Oh whoops! Silly me! That was tomorrow!

I sighed, rubbing my hand down the side of my face. I couldn't handle the group chats half the time.

A peppy ding emanated from my phone, and I glanced at the new message.

Natalie:
Morning!

Me:
What's up Nat?

Natalie:
Nothing much, A. Remember that lit club got canceled

Me:
Again? That's like the 5th time

Natalie:

Well, the librarian keeps getting sick lmao

Me:
Ha. Alright, I gtg

Natalie:
Bye!

I blinked, my eyes slowly adjusting to the room. Sighing, I pulled off my dark purple comforter. I tried to urge myself to get up as I yawned, shaking off the breeze the fan sent my way.

My feet touched the well-worn *My Little Pony* rug. It was something I hadn't played with in years, but the rug lived on. I stretched my arms above my head and picked up my phone again, a slight crack embedded in the screen. I looked at the other group chats, but there weren't many to check. I would have texted something, but then they would realize I was still added to the chat, and then they would probably remove me.

I turned to the desk sitting next to my bed, pressing my face against my shiny vanity mirror to check if there was any acne. Not surprisingly, there was, but hopefully, people didn't notice. I just wanted to be rid of it, but alas. Then I turned my body to the side and looked at my tall, thin frame with its pipe cleaner arms. I wasn't any supermodel, but I guessed I looked fine, given that I was only thirteen. I still checked every day, just in case, though.

Grabbing my phone, I walked out of the room, not expecting the light in the hallway to be on. I blinked a few times before the spots faded away, noticing the bathroom door ajar.

My older sister Gwen was brushing her teeth in the bathroom we shared. She caught sight of me in the mirror, turning to me. "Oh. Hey Alex. Sleep well?" she asked.

"Yeah, I guess." I held up my phone. "Group chats got me up."

"Tell me about it," she said, sighing.

She continued brushing her teeth, and the smell of minty toothpaste was potent in the air. I noticed her hair was up high in a towel.

"Hey, you look like a chubby narwhal," I said jokingly, as a stupid grin spread across my face.

Gwen's eyes went wide.

My heart started to race, as I realized I did it again. "Oh my gosh! I didn't mean it like tha—"

She closed her eyes and exhaled slowly, focusing on her breath.

She took a calm breath in before speaking. "It's okay. I know you were just kidding."

Gwen smiled a little and chuckled. For a second, I thought she was going to scold me and say my full name like our parents.

Besides, my full name was rather disappointing, in my opinion. It was "Alexandra," but it didn't sound anything like me. And I wasn't choosing the name *Alexa* any time soon or *Alexia* either. It sounded like the name of someone who was trying way too hard to be popular. I probably shouldn't have said that. I once said that to someone when I was introducing myself, and then she said, "I'm Alexia." Then I babbled on that it was a fine name for her but just not a good one for me. I added that she really was a pretty Alexia, but I'd be weird with it. That's when she just walked away from me. It was weird when I saw her in gym class. If I said, "Hi, Alexia," then she looked at me like I was making fun of her name. And if I didn't say her name, then it felt like I was avoiding it. That was three years ago, and I was still trying to avoid her even though she started using her middle name, Lisa.

Wait. Maybe that was my fault?

Thankfully, I was good at texting, but talking just wasn't my forte. My mouth just always ran. But it made for some good laughs. At least the embarrassment paid off in some way or another. Sometimes it was hard being the butt of the joke, though. Sometimes it seemed like I would never be more than that.

Just a bad punchline.

I steeled my laughter, grabbing a nearby comb. After easing my hair's frizz with it, I quickly brushed my teeth. Back in my room, I grabbed a blank dry-fit shirt from my closet and slipped on a pair of wrinkled jeggings from the back of my drawer. When I got to the dining table, avocado toast and a bowl of cheerios were waiting for me. I smiled. Gwen always knew my favorites, although simple. Then I realized I brushed my teeth before eating. Shoot. At least there wasn't orange juice. But I didn't have a problem with minty-tasting cereal.

"Hey, Mom?" I called before realizing my parents weren't home.

Mom and Dad's shifts at the hospital meant they were often gone before we woke up, so Gwen made me breakfast every morning and looked after me during the week. She filled in as a parent, even though she was only four years older than me.

I sat down in the dining room chair, my back pressed against the hard wooden backing. The table was cluttered with papers and files where my parents sat. I took a bite of the cereal with the spoon Gwen put in. I quickly finished the sweet-tasting cereal before taking bites of the toast.

"Did you finish *Catching Fire* for English?" Gwen asked as soon as I shoved a piece of toast in my mouth.

"MmmHhmm," I tried to say. "Next up is the one for Sherlock. Do you have a copy? It's for *Hound of the Baskervilles*," I asked.

I grabbed the plates as I walked towards the kitchen, my bare feet brushing against the cold tile.

Gwen also grabbed her finished plate, standing. "I didn't read that one. I had Ms. Crowne that year. Just add it to the cart, and mom will place the order this week."

I placed my dishes into the dishwasher as I began to make my lunch, grabbing a slice of bread and a jar of extra crunchy peanut butter. While I spread the peanut butter, Gwen grabbed a container of lettuce for her Caesar salad.

"Hey Alex, see this," she said, handing me her phone.

It was the *Instagram* for my school. It was early in the school year, but with nothing interesting in Greentree, *The Week event* was *everything*. Every mid-November, the middle school had special events right before Thanksgiving break. It kicked off with some sporting events, and everyone was excused from class to watch. They brought in food trucks as well, which were always much better than the school lunch. Midweek was a field trip to an amusement park that also had a mini-zoo built in. It was a big field trip spot, but it was still fun to go to nevertheless. Saturday was *The Dance*. Even though it was in the cafeteria, everyone thought of it as a middle school prom. All the gossip of who's dating who always came out during 'The Week,' so the drama factor was intense.

"You know I can't wait!" I said excitedly, my eyes brightening slightly.

"Yeah, yeah. When I went to Birchwood, *The Week* was the best," she said, reminiscing fondly.

I glanced at the clock, drawing my eyes away from her.

"Oh shoot! I gotta go! Lock the door, please!" I said, packing the last of my things into my backpack.

"Will do!" Gwen called. "See you later!"

"Bye!" I replied as I hastily grabbed a jacket, pushing open the forest-green surface of the door.

A chilly morning breeze greeted me, and the click of the lock sounded behind me. I shivered into my well-worn dusty blue jacket as the sun created a colorful blanket of purples and scarlets. I stared at the sight for a minute before I shivered again, stripping the moment away. I wanted to remember the colors so I could draw them later. But, I despised cold fronts and how they could just ruin your day, through both the cold, and through learning about them in science class. Nevertheless, the bitter cold made the light film of sun on my face feel better than usual.

I turned the corner and brushed my hand on the chain-link fence. It rattled my fingers in a soothing way, calming my nerves slightly. After a while of doing this, I saw a figure up ahead. My heart jumped a little, a smile spreading on my face as I began to walk faster. I'd recognize their silhouette anywhere.

"Hey, Angel, wait up!" I yelled after her.

She turned around, and her eyes met mine. They were a pale green—not hazel or even a blue-green. I usually didn't pay attention to that stuff, but it was hard to miss Angel's thin, vibrant eyes. She calmly paused, waiting for me to catch up as a soft smile rested on her face.

"Hey, Alex," she said. "How are you?"

She looked up at me a little, her flute case swinging by her side.

I looked away from the case. It always made me jealous of her. Not because I wanted a flute but because she had so many friends in band class.

They always went on trips, had sleepovers, and just had fun. And I wasn't ever part of that group. I dropped out of band because I felt out of place there, but now not being in band made me feel even more out of place.

"I'm good," I smiled. "You?"

"Same," she replied, beginning to pick at her nails. "Oh, I figured out how to get the custom painting mod for *Minecraft* you were asking about."

"Really?"

She nodded her head. "After I finished coding the Magic mod, I found this website where you literally just have to insert the pictures and download the pack, and BOOM. Your photos are in the game."

"I will never figure out how you do that. You are the best!"

"Hey. Are my hands cold?" Angel asked.

It was an unusual question, but I took hold of her hands anyways. Her hands were indeed warm despite the cool weather.

"No," I said. "They're hot, well, um … not like *hot* hot … I mean a boy might say that about you but … uh … not me … oh um … sorry … that was a little offensive … and heteronormative … anyway gotta go bye!"

Yikes. I tried to rush past her, leaving the embarrassment behind.

She grabbed my elbow before I darted away.

"Hey. Alex. It's fine. You're my best friend," she said.

I started blushing. "Yeah … sorry about that …"

It was way more embarrassing when I tried to flee.

We walked in silence, my face still hot from my stupidity. Being quiet was one of Angel's favorite hobbies, and currently, one of mine as well.

"Oh, did you get that image I emailed you?" she asked.

"Mhm, I didn't check," I said, pulling out my phone.

I scrolled through and clicked on the link. It was an image of another mod she created in *Minecraft*.

"Stop showing off," I teased, a smile on my face.

Angel beamed just for a second. "So, are you going to log onto the server tonight?"

"Probably. But if not, I'll be able to get on tomorrow."

Angel nodded, seemingly pleased with that response.

At the beginning of the year, Angel had started a schoolwide *Minecraft* server for anyone with the game at home. Somehow, she was able to get it cross-platform so almost anyone could play. It was an easy way to bond after school, so most people had joined.

She smiled, brushing her short black hair out of her face. The sign for our school came into view.

BIRCHWOOD MIDDLE SCHOOL EST 1987

Orange and brown leaves crunched under my feet as Angel and I entered the campus. It was a fairly average place like somewhere you could pass by and not notice, which was typical for Greentree. We entered through the metal gates on the side of the school, just recently unlocked. The brick buildings with red metal roofs cast shade over the concrete as Angel and I walked side by side. A few passersby gathered nearby, waiting for the band room to open so they could put away their instruments.

And yet again, the pang of loneliness struck. Band wasn't really for me after I checked it out in sixth grade since none of the instruments fit, and none of the people got along with me. I had just decided to do PE instead. But I was just as out of place in PE as I was in band.

Another nearby group was giggling over a person's shoulder, eyes locked on their phone. But the air of silence still coated the school like a thick blanket, only ready to be pulled off once the bell rang. I walked up a ramp, turned the corner, and pushed open the metal and plastic door to enter the air-conditioned hallway lined with lockers. Angel went to the side of the hallway, unlocked her locker, and shoved in her books.

I went the other way, doing the same. As the locker shut closed, I saw Angel beginning to walk out towards the library, her small stature bobbing up and down as she strolled through the campus.

"Come on," she called out.

I followed her back into the open quad as she went towards the library. Just like the rest of the school, the library was quaint but much quieter than any other place. It wasn't marble floors and a golden ceiling or a rickety old shack either. It had thick navy carpeting and wooden desks, walls, and shelves lined with books. Posters and art from classes sat on top of shelves, adding more color to the room. Angel and I walked towards our table nestled between the fantasy and realistic fiction shelves where the others were already sitting. Natalie had her face in a book, as usual.

"Hey Nat," Angel said, sitting down.

Natalie looked up, smiling.

"Yeah, hey you … wait, that doesn't sound right. Uum, hi, Nat. I'm sorry, I meant to say hey Nat to begin with—" I said, fumbling over my words.

"Alex, sit down," Natalie said, a hint of amusement in her voice. "It's fine."

"Oh, yeah, where do I sit—oh, right here's fine then," I said, struggling to find a seat.

I finally sat down, sweating a little from the experience.

I noticed Angel was looking at me, holding in a laugh.

"What?" I asked.

I turned to Natalie and I noticed both were trying not to laugh.

And there I went, running my mouth.

Natalie looked back at her book, completely absorbed within a matter of seconds. I got up from my chair to stand behind her, almost running into a bookshelf on the way there. I carefully put my hand on her shoulder, making her jump in her seat.

"Oh my god," she sighed, turning around. "You scared me."

I shoved my hands into my pockets. "Oh, I'm so sorry … I just wanted to—"

"It's fine, Alex," Natalie said, chuckling.

"What book is that?" I asked, switching the subject.

"*Red Queen,*" she said. "Actually, it's the last book in the series. I've been working through the YA section recently."

"You have like thirty pages left."

"Yeah … this one has multiple voices, so it slowed me down. I started Saturday."

"You're ridiculous," I sighed, walking back to my seat.

This time I actually did run into the bookshelf.

"Ah, god!" I said loudly as I banged my toe.

"Shhh!" The librarian hissed.

She went back to her dusty manuscript, her cat-eyed glasses perched on top of her bony-looking nose.

Natalie looked up again, panicked. "Crap, Alex, are you alright?"

"Alex, did you …?" Angel asked.

"I'm fine … I'm such a klutz, I'm so so sorry," I said, my voice high-pitched as I spoke, limping back to my seat.

"Alright," Angel said, still slightly concerned.

"Hey, did you read the new chapter of my fanfic? It's fine if you didn't; it came out a few days ago," Natalie said, putting down her book for a second.

I nodded. "It was really good. I really liked it when, um … I know I read it the day it came out … um," I said, racking my brain for something to say.

I looked at random places around the room to figure something out. I felt like a movie character trying to get out of murder.

Natalie raised her eyebrows playfully.

I finally came up with something after a few seconds too long. "Oh yeah! I loved it when Ellora just betrayed everyone. Cordelia never even saw it coming," I breathed a sigh of relief.

She smiled. "Glad you liked it. Just happy that *Tyrants* is a good fandom. And that betrayal scene took me like three weeks to come up with."

"Oh, cool! You're such a good writer, so I'm really glad that you could join the fandom. It took me forever to find, and I'm super glad it paid off. Because honestly, the animatics are so good and—"

"Alex, you're rambling."

"Oh, sorry," I said, slinking back into my seat.

"No, no!" Natalie said. "But that's okay; I just wanted you to be aware or something, but that's totally fine!"

I smiled, perking up after a few seconds. "Hey, did you catch last night's stream?"

My toe began to throb, so I slipped off my shoe. Was it starting to swell? That couldn't be good.

"Yeah. But there were only like 100 viewers! It's such an underrated fandom!" Natalie complained, sinking into her seat.

"*Harry Potter* has like a million fics for all of their ships!" [who is speaking?]

I sighed, continuing to assess my injury. "Honestly, *Tyrants* deserves a much larger fanbase.

"At this point, I've been so content-starved I decided to make my own fics," Natalie laughed.

"As the great Ellora said right before she died tragically, 'You're on your own now, so do it yourself,'" I said.

"Noooo!" Natalie said, cupping her face with her hands. "Not the quote! It always gets me."

"So … is this English or fandom? I'm very confused," Angel said, glancing at us.

"Fandom. Sorry about that," Natalie grinned. "I wish you had *YouTube* so you could watch the videos for it."

"I want to join so badly!" Angel said. "But my parents restricted all my devices. So, if you don't mind me asking, what exactly is the *Tyrants* fandom? I know a few tidbits and that it's a *Minecraft YouTuber* fandom, but you haven't said much else."

I smiled, excitement bubbling inside me. "Oh, you have so much to learn."

Natalie seemed excited too. "The *Tyrants* fandom is based off of a few different *Minecraft* streamers who build their own kingdoms, but as it went on, the leaders became more and more corrupt, leading to a bit of humor as well as some interesting characters in their roleplay."

"For example," I said, continuing. "Ellora Oversight. She's a character in the fandom who rules a kingdom inside an underground ravine, making her living off of the imports of her nation. But she began a witch guild and betrayed her best friend, Cordelia, for her ultimate power. Not to ment—"

I stopped talking as I heard the door open behind me. I turned around, craning my neck to see who had walked in.

My heart skipped a beat, my face going hot.

Thomas.

"Hey guys, what'd I miss?"

I had no clue why I felt such a burning feeling when I looked at him. I knew him for most of elementary school, but sometime in the past year, he grew four inches and became way taller than me. He had his braces taken off and joined the swim team. It was like he had completely changed on the outside, but he was still Thomas. He still had that same smile that still managed to give me butterflies whenever I saw it. After that, I started to find myself glancing at him in class and being *way* more nervous around him. Gwen said I had a full-on crush, but I couldn't tell my friends. There was no way I would ever do that.

"Nothing much," Angel said, now at a nearby shelf, picking out a book.

Thomas sat down next to me, pulling out his phone, and adjusting his black-rimmed glasses.

"Hurt yourself again?" he said, nodding to the foot I was still cradling in my lap.

"Oh yeah … bookcase was possessed, and it … um kicked me." I slipped my shoe back on.

My heart skipped quite a few more beats, but I tried to busy myself with something other than picking my nails.

Thomas grinned at me before turning away.

"What book is that?" he asked Natalie.

I spaced out a bit as the conversation repeated itself. I pulled out my sketchbook to work on the fanart I had started a few days ago. My pencil brushed against the paper, marking its past movements. I added the signature masquerade mask onto the character, finishing the lace around the mask's edges. I always thought the style of the *Tyrants* fandom was unique. Everyone wore masquerade masks or formal clothing throughout the series, and it was a distinct style that I had fallen in love with. I moved my pencil to add the folds of the outfit when I heard a voice.

"That's pretty good," Natalie said, leaning over my shoulder, smiling. "Can you draw me?" she asked carefully.

"Well, I would, but it's almost time for the bell to ring. And I'm not that good anyway—"

I heard the ear-piercing screech of the bell across campus.

Shoot.

I snapped my sketchbook shut, rushing to pack up my supplies as the others left for class. I grabbed my backpack, running to catch up with them. The hallways always looked the same throughout the school, with classic over-polished linoleum and harsh white lights. The place would have seemed like a maze if it wasn't for the classrooms interrupting the never-ending hall every so often. I walked into homeroom, closing the wooden door as I entered.

The classroom was cluttered with papers and newly discarded pencils on the floor. We were only in the second quarter, and everything was already messy. I couldn't say I expected any less. I sat my backpack on my desk and attempted to weave my way through to find my friends.

Emphasis on attempting.

After I clumsily walked through the rows of desks, I saw my friends in a little cluster at the front of the classroom.

They were all seated next to one another. We had our seats changed for like the fourth time in the past two weeks, and it was always so senseless.

"Hey, guys!" I called.

"Hey!" Thomas said in response, waving a little.

His eyes were deep and velvety, like a warm cup of hot chocolate. Maybe prolonged eye contact wasn't a great idea, but I couldn't really help it.

I hadn't noticed the heat in my cheeks until I heard a giggle nearby.

"Hey Alex! Do you remember when you got cracker crumbs in your bra in fifth grade? That was *so* funny," Perry sneered.

She made a side glance at her friend.

My head whipped around at them, my eyes widened, and I swallowed hard.

Perry and Brit. They were new to my friend group, but I wasn't too close to them. Perry was gossipy and sometimes flat-out rude, and Brit was oblivious, but usually, she was tolerable. My friends liked hanging out with them, so I had to deal with their drama.

But to add insult to injury, we didn't even go to the same school in fifth grade.

"Hey. You remember when you were too tall for the water fountain, and you squatted really short to drink?" Thomas laughed. "That was really creative."

My stomach twisted into knots.

"Umm … yeah," I fake-laughed.

He was never going to like me. How could I be so dumb? I couldn't even look him in the eye; I was so nervous. I looked down and walked over to my newly assigned seat, sighing.

Everyone ignored the school announcements except for the auburn-haired, popular girl who seemed to be paying attention and writing things in her planner. I started to pick at my cuticles, upset about the embarrassing stories. When the bell rang, we all rushed out into the wide halls.

Thomas tapped my shoulder as I turned around to look at him.

"Yeah?" I asked.

I started blushing. Why did I say *yeah?* Was that stupid? Why were there so many butterflies—?

"I just wanted to say sorry for saying that earlier," Thomas commented. "You, um, seemed a little uncomfortable? I didn't mean whatever you thought I meant; I just thought the whole water fountain thing was cute, but you seemed a little panicked, so? I don't know if that makes sense or not—"

"Nope," I said. I could feel my palms sweating. "You don't have to say sorry at all."

He thought I was cute?

I didn't know I could blush that hard …

Thomas smiled, but the conversation stopped abruptly when the halls started swarming with people.

The halls were almost never that full. We were elbow to elbow, jammed against the cool metal of the lockers as people cascaded through, bringing a parade of discordant chatter with them. I made eye contact with the others, and it was obvious we were all thinking the exact same thing.

The Pops.

The clique of girls that ruled our middle school with an iron fist.

"Who do they think they are?" Natalie rolled her eyes in disgust as the others caught up.

We all gave looks of agreement.

Underneath the cold artificial light, a crowd of people swarmed the hallways. The crowd, all grades alike, were shoving and pushing to get to the front.

Because at the very front, leading the pack, was none other than the queen of the seventh grade.

Charlene West.

Charlene flipped her long, dark, chocolate-brown hair out of her flawless, beach-tanned face. Her jean shorts looked slightly too tight, and her white t-shirt with an embroidered design seemed to shout popular. A cream-colored coat was draped over her shoulders, and she didn't even seem to be paying attention to the crowd. Instead, she was applying another layer of her bubblegum pink lipstick while looking in a compact mirror.

I never wore makeup, but even I knew that applying it while walking was a feat.

"Out of the way, people! Give Charlene some room!" A voice yelled, sounding like they owned the place.

I glanced at the speaker who said it. She trailed behind Charlene, scoffing at the crowds behind her. She crossed her arms, whispering with a smug grin on her face to a few others in the group.

"I hate Ava," Angel said, referring to the girl. "You know she must get her blonde hair dyed every week. I mean, her eyebrows are brown."

She wasn't wrong about that.

"I don't really think Mallory's as smart as she looks," Perry commented jokingly, nodding toward the auburn one from my homeroom class.

Brit bounced over, marveling at *The Pops* passing by.

"She is," I said. "I've seen her compete in math competitions. She always gets the highest score out of everyone."

Perry pressed her lips together as she looked back.

I was right, though. Mallory was known as the *smart one* out of *The Pops*. She certainly looked smart with her teal glasses perched on her tiny nose and olive skin. She would be pretty, except her mouth was almost always pinched tightly, as if you were wasting her time just by being near her.

I noticed one of them was striding towards the front, trying to get the most of the attention, smiling brightly for the show, but still careful to not go ahead of Charlene. Nina. Of course.

While Charlene was pretty, Nina was gorgeous. No one in middle school should have been so genetically perfect. The boys even renamed their main group chat *Nina Fanboy Club*. And she loved it. Her ice-blue eyes, dark skin, and inky black hair looked stunningly beautiful, and her smile rivaled even Charlene's. Last week her hair had been in Bantu knots, but now she had taken them out, and her hair had spiral curls.

"You know, they really all do look like lollipops," Thomas said. "They all have different colored hair."

"And sticks for legs," I chuckled.

Natalie snorted, and we all started howling with laughter.

"It's so ridiculous that our school is like a teen movie," Angel said.

"Yeah. This school is basically a Disney teen movie, except there are considerably less adult actors," I replied.

"Facts," Natalie chimed. "It's basically *High School Musical* except without singing."

"Oh my god, imagine if *The Pops* spontaneously burst into song. That would make my year," Angel commented.

"What would make my year is if Ryan Reynolds showed up," Thomas joked.

Brit laughed at that, and the rest of us started laughing along with her.

It took a while for *The Pops* to make it out of range; the crowd following them was huge. I was so glad I no longer *crowded* because the last time I tried crowding was a trainwreck.

"I like your outfit, Charlene. Where'd you get it?" I had asked.

She had responded with a scoff, sneering as she spoke, "It's couture. My parents got it for me in New York. You can't get it because you don't know the right people."

After that, I didn't try to crowd. I rolled my eyes whenever they passed, trying to ignore the sting of embarrassment that still lingered.

After *The Pops* had cleared the hall, I continued my way to first period, a few of my friends following behind me as we walked there. I entered the room, took my seat, and pulled out my folder and supplies.

Mrs. Esma's civics class was uneventful. But I overheard *The Pops* talking about a party they had on the previous Saturday. I hunched down in my seat. I would never be able to throw a party and expect people to come. Heck, it would be fun to just *go* to a party. But not everyone got what they wanted, so I enjoyed the time spent playing *Minecraft* or watching *Tyrants* with my friends.

I checked my phone after I had finished my work. Mrs. Esma always let us pull out our phones when we had completed the lesson. There weren't any messages for me, just some stories on *Insta*. I started walking towards my reading class when we were dismissed. In the hallway, I caught a brief glimpse of Nina. She was hand in hand with Red, her boyfriend. With his beaming smile and dark springy coils, he matched her in attractiveness. I couldn't understand how anyone could look so flawless and confident in seventh grade. They made the rest of us look like we didn't come out of the oven correctly.

I walked through the halls, spotting the door with a paper sign on it reading, *Mrs. Valerie.*

I opened the heavy dark blue door, the cold of it seeping into my fingers. The room was unnaturally bright because of the white artificial lights that every school had, making it akin to an interrogation room. There were a few colorful decorations adorning the walls saying things like, "Reading is fun!" and "Missspewling is bad" and other cheesy statements like that.

I walked over to my usual desk and began to sit down like every other day.

"Hey! That's my seat!" someone called.

"What do you mean?" I asked. "This is my seat. I've always sat here."

I found the person who the voice belonged to. They were short and squat, with unbrushed, frizzy hair. The light blended with it, making it hard to tell what their original hair color was. My hair looked nothing like that, being a hazelnut brown, which was slightly lighter than Thomas's.

"Sorry. The seats changed. Mrs. V said so," the girl said, pointing over to Mrs. Valerie.

The teacher did not look up from her desk, looking questioningly at some of the papers she pulled from the neat stacks arranged there. She pulled her dark golden-brown hair into a slim ponytail, typing something on her computer shortly afterward.

"Oh, I'm so sorry. I didn't know; I'll just go," I said, stuttering a little.

I looked at the dry-erase board, finally noticing the seating chart written in an oversaturated blue marker. I stared at it for a few seconds, sighing in defeat as I turned my head to where I would be sitting from now on.

Oh, no.

One of them propped her feet on top of her desk, blowing a thick strand of her sleek leather black hair out of her face. The other girl was pressing buttons on her phone, giggling in the process.

I did have the urge to tell her that having a phone wasn't allowed, but I resisted.

I sat down between them silently. The girl with her feet on the desk glanced at me, sighing dramatically as she crossed her arms.

"Hi, Perry," I said shakily as she looked at me.

"Hey," she said flatly, not returning the look.

"Oh hey," The other said, her eyes brightening.

"Hi, Brit," I said, looking at her.

Of course, I had to sit between them. It was like the world wanted to destroy me.

"How have you been?" Brit asked, gently placing her phone on the table, her long, pink-painted nails shining softly in the light.

"Good? I guess," I said.

I did not want to be in this conversation. For some reason, the two of them always made me uncomfortable. Even more uncomfortable when they were both together.

"Hey, are you still in that weird fandom phase of yours?" Perry asked, bored, glancing over at Brit.

"It's not weird," I replied.

I gritted my teeth a little. That *weird fandom phase* was the Tyrants fandom. So no, I was not out of that phase, and it was none of her business.

"Oh. Whatever," she said, grabbing her bag from the floor. She slipped out a small box. "Want some gum?" she asked, holding it out to me.

"I'm good," I said, slinking into my chair.

Perry offered it to Brit, who reached across my face and gladly grabbed a piece.

"So," Brit said, chewing the gum. "Anything new lately? I haven't caught up with you recently," Brit said, beginning to blow a bubble.

"Um, no. Nothing new with me," I said.

In all honesty, I was purposely trying to ignore Brit.

Perry scoffed. "Told you, Brit. She doesn't have anything to say."

"That's a little rude—" I started, but Perry cut me off.

"Did you know Charlene and her friends are having a party this weekend?" she said, looking at Brit.

She looked directly past me, just like I was invisible.

"Oh my gosh, really?" Brit chirped, her eyes widening.

Perry slipped out her phone and handed it to Brit to let her read the message. Brit's tan skin glowed a dim blue in the light of the phone as she skimmed it.

I sighed, turning away from them. I glanced over at *The Pops* for a second. Only Charlene, Ava, and Nina were in my reading class, but Angel was seated next to Ava, who was currently showing Angel some texts and giggling wildly. From what I could tell, Angel didn't seem to be liking the new seating arrangement.

Poor Angel.

"That's so cool!" Brit said, handing the phone back to Perry.

I could see something of a grin flash across Perry's face, but her eyes turned downward as she quickly slipped her phone back into her bag. Her grin faded as fast as it came, her mouth twisting back into its usual straight line.

"Alright, class! Today we're going over how to write an essay," Mrs. Valerie announced, walking to the front of the board.

"Ooh!" Brit said, turning to me. "Call me later, K?"

"I think we're having a group call tomorrow, right?" I asked. "We could just talk then."

Brit nodded, unfazed. "Yep! You're right. We'll talk then!"

I seethed inside. Perry always seemed to be rude to me when others weren't around. She would say something just mean enough to tick me off, and if I challenged her, she would say that she was joking and I needed to stop being so sensitive. And Brit? Well, she tried. That didn't mean I liked her. She was oblivious, aloof, airheaded. Gossipy. All I knew was that I didn't like them. Or trust them.

After drowning out Mrs. Valerie for fifty minutes, I rushed to math, being the first to arrive. I was in the eighth-grade honors Algebra, so none of my friends were in the class with me. Most of them had a lower-level course, and I was the only seventh grader in my class, so even *The Pops* weren't there. Not even Mallory, who was so advanced she was doing virtual school for Geometry.

Our daily math equation was on the board in neat handwriting. Under it was a picture of Albert Einstein and his greatest work. Even though he was a scientist, he was still a fantastic mathematician, which was what I hoped I would be someday. I sat down and started on the daily problem. It was slope, one of my strong suits.

Numbers dripped from my hand onto my paper, creating a masterpiece of an equation. Numbers always felt new and exciting, no matter how long I had known them. When I was a kid, I liked to imagine each number had a different personality. One was lonely, three was weird, and fifteen was beautiful, nice, funny, and exciting. I've always liked the number fifteen. It felt like a perfect balance to me. I kept writing my intricate notes on my paper with expert skill. I double-checked myself. Right. Yet again. I sighed happily. That's what I loved. I wrote down my numbers, and then I did it again, and I was right. I was always right. I loved being right. I hoped to keep it that way. Math meant no awkwardness, no judgment, no tripping, no blushing.

A few more people arrived, and Mr. Koffman approached the whiteboard and began teaching.

"Alright, class," Mr. Koffman said, his voice booming throughout the classroom. "Welcome to another Tuesday. Will everyone pass forward their homework, please?"

We all passed forward our sheets, filled to the brim with complex equations.

"Has everyone done their Bellringer yet?" he inquired.

We all nodded our heads, except for the select few that were late and still scribbling the rest of the problem in a messy haste.

"Good," he said. "Now, would anyone like to demonstrate?"

My hand shot up fast. A few others popped up shortly after, but I had already made my mark.

Mr. Koffman pointed at my raised hand. "Alex, would you like to come up to the board to show us?" he asked.

"Sure!" I said energetically.

I stood up from my seat and walked toward the whiteboard. I grabbed a magenta dry-erase marker and spread my hand across the board. I displayed the detailed steps of the process in a matter of seconds, letting all my feelings go into the numbers. With a few more slashes of my marker, the masterpiece of numerical equations was finished.

The class started double-checking their work to see if I was accurate.

After a few seconds of silence and scribbling on paper, one person raised their hand.

"Yes?" I asked.

"But wouldn't it be fifty-one? Wouldn't you divide the first number and plug the other one in its place?"

"I don't think so," I said. "The formula was 'y equals slope times x, plus the y-intercept.' And if you follow all those steps in order, you would get fourteen."

The person looked down at their paper and redid the math.

When they finished, they raised their head and said, "You're right. I got it now."

Mr. Koffman nodded in approval. I walked back to my seat, and I passed two eighth graders on the math team, Raaj and Jay. Raaj held out his hand. I stood there, staring at it.

"What?" I asked.

"High-five," he said.

"Oh, I thought you meant talk to the hand."

"Just hit. I kinda feel like an idiot," he grinned.

"Oh, yeah, sorry." I high-fived him, and I cringed in my mind at my own stupidity.

Mr. Koffman gave us another equation to solve, and soon enough, we were off in our heads, piecing together the puzzles put in front of us and just solving away like we were playing video games.

The bell rang, and I walked through the halls to the cafeteria.

"Hey, Alex!" I heard Raaj say behind me.

I skidded to a halt and turned around. "Oh hey."

"So, I know you're not on the math team, but do you want to come over on Saturday and help me practice for the next competition?" he asked. "Jay will be there too, by the way. It's at my house. I'll DM you the address if you want to come."

"Oh, yeah, sure. What time?"

"Maybe 5:00. Sound good?"

"Yeah, definitely," I replied with a smile.

"Great, I'll see you then."

"See you!"

I rushed to the lunchroom, but I hated to leave math class. It was the one thing that made me want to wake up in the morning, but at least I could do some extra math on Saturday. Maybe with enough practice, I would be brave enough to try out for the team.

I walked through the cafeteria's large open doorway and caught a glimpse of Nina flirting with Red. Mallory stood next to her, rolling her eyes. I had overheard through gossip that *The Pops* were desperately trying to set her up, but she just never seemed interested.

People started cramming around Nina and Mallory, trying to find out details of the upcoming party. I rolled my eyes, walking further into the cafeteria and picking a seat close to Thomas.

Unfortunately, The Queen Bee and her minions sat right next to me.

"Could you please move?" Ava asked politely, moving a curl of her blonde hair away from her face. I could see Thomas transfixed on her and my head started to pound. My jaw tightened, and I felt a rising irritation that I had never felt before.

"Um … no." I said flatly.

I didn't understand why they were on this side of the cafeteria until I looked over and saw that a ceiling tile had collapsed from a water leak. Several of the cafeteria tables were blocked off while the janitor worked to clean them up.

"Just get out of the way, weirdo," Mallory said, pushing her glasses up on her nose.

I sighed, a frown now on my face. This was the table I always sat at, and I wasn't going to let them annoy me into moving. I stood my ground, and after a few minutes, they got fed up, moving towards some empty seats and stealing them before the rest of my friends could sit down. I was uncomfortable that they were sitting next to me, especially because they were whispering the whole time, and I couldn't eavesdrop. I turned my back to them and talked with Thomas.

"You excited about next week?" I asked him, pulling my *Lays* chips out.

He began to unwrap a sandwich. "Yeah. But I wish they had swimming instead of just track events next week. I would do so much better." Thomas commented.

I struggled to open my chips. "Oh yeah … that's true. But we don't have a pool. Where do you practice?"

My chip bag seemed to be superglued. Why must my food mock me?

"At the *400 Club* near my place." Thomas reached over and took the chip bag out of my hand. He opened it with ease and gave it back to me without pausing. "Thank goodness it's heated. Because I'm there almost every morning at 6am."

"Holy hell, Thomas. That's so early! Thanks," I said, indicating my chips.

I pulled out my own sandwich.

A while later, I noticed that Nina went running for the bathroom. I didn't think too much of it; she probably just had to go. As for me, I just waited and kept eating my peanut butter sandwich. I liked the soft bread and the nutty paste that stuck to my mouth.

After a few more minutes of talking, Nina came rushing back to the table. When she sat down, she popped a tablet of gum into her mouth and was soon caught up in the conversations of her friends.

The bell rang again, and we walked to science class. I took my seat next to Natalie and Angel, as usual. We weren't paying attention to the board, which was set up with notes about different types of rocks. I wasn't a big fan of Mrs. Harlem's teaching method—which consisted of plastering notes to the board as our only means of education. I never wanted to be disrespectful to her, but she always taught us basic things and was just foul about everything.

None of us really cared about what she was saying; we already knew all of it. Even Mallory, who was probably the most attentive, was rolling her eyes.

Natalie turned her head to face Angel on the other side of me and whispered, "Hey Angel did you see that show last ni—"

I cut her off, remembering something really cool. "Hey! So, last night I was playing *Animal Crossing*, and the—" I started excitedly.

Angel stopped me from saying anything else, "Hey, um, Natalie was talking. I don't mean to be rude or anything, but I want her to finish."

I just wanted to have a portal to another dimension open up underneath me. "Oh yeah … sorry."

"No, no! It's fine; just wait a few minutes, okay?" Natalie said.

I slunk into my seat, nodding. Gwen defined my awkwardness as *missing social cues,* and most of the time, that definition was spot on.

With no one to talk to, I started listening to the frenzy at hand.

"Nina! Take that gum out of your mouth!" Mrs. Harlem barked.

"I'm sorry, Mrs. Harlem, I can't do that," she twirled a lock of hair on her finger. "I just don't want my breath to smell after lunch."

"That's no excuse to be chewing gum. Go to the dean's office," Mrs. Harlem commanded.

She ripped off a pink hall pass and handed it to Nina. Nina scoffed but took the slip. Mrs. Harlem was the only teacher that didn't like her. Then again, Mrs. Harlem did not seem to like anyone.

I glanced at Angel and Natalie. I didn't quite understand the punishment since it didn't match the crime at all. Although I didn't like Nina, getting sent to the dean's office for chewing gum was just moronic. Mrs. Harlem just seemed off the rails sometimes.

Nina walked out, sighing as she went on her way. Luckily the dean liked her; she would probably go scot-free despite Mrs. Harlem's strongly worded complaint.

After fifty more minutes of torture and several exchanges of notes, the shrill sound of the bell spread relief throughout the room.

I slumped through the hallway, dragging myself to the locker room. I seriously regretted signing up for PE. Every popular person and wannabee was in the class, but none of my friends. So, there I was, not fitting in. Except this time, I didn't fit in while wearing a stupid gym uniform with my gangling arms and legs sticking out. Not to mention, I wasn't the best at sports. It was sweaty and tiring, and I wasn't good at any aspect of it. I often wondered if I should've switched back to band with its spit pads and reeds.

While back in the locker room after class, I heard a ping from my phone. Even though phones weren't allowed, I discreetly pulled it out while nobody was around.

Angel:
Any injuries today?

Me:
I successfully avoided getting smacked in the face. Although some cowardice was involved.

Angel:
As I would expect

Me:
Excuse me, what do you mean by that?

Angel:
You = Coward

Me:
Hey!
Only I can use self-deprecation!

Angel:
Ha
I assume you're doing dodgeball?

Me:
>:(Yes. If Shakespeare had this class, even he would have said: What fresh hell is this.

Angel:
xD I think that was Dorothy Parker tho

Me:
Who?

Angel:
I'll pull up some of her poetry and send it later. Cya :)

I quickly put on the rest of my clothes in haste. My last class was writing, and since the essay practice was a waste of time, I mainly zoned out.

"Hey, Natalie?" I whispered.

"Yeah?" she mouthed from a seat away.

"I'm so sorry I interrupted you earlier."

"Alex, chill; it's been like three hours. You don't need to worry about that."

"Bu—"

"It's fine, Alex. You're doing that thing again when you focus on past mistakes."

I slunk into my seat, kind of embarrassed again.

When the bell rang for the last time, I walked back home. No one was walking with me, but that was normal. A lot of my friends had after-school activities, but I hadn't found anything that I wanted to be involved in. I had wanted the math team, but I didn't know if I was good enough for it. And besides, my parents were too busy to drive me to anything, and Gwen was usually busy as well.

It was blazing hot, and I was sweating, much to my dismay. I really regretted wearing jeggings on a day like this.

Although I wanted to get home and change clothes, I had a craving for something sweet.

And like the world read my mind, I saw a small candy shop around the corner.

I hadn't noticed the place before, but I could see why. It was relatively small, shrouded in foliage, its appearance quaint and inviting, like a warm cabin in a blizzard.

I crossed the street as the sun streaked through the leaves surrounding the small building. There was a dilapidated sign on the top with a store name that I couldn't quite read. But the place's lights were on despite the abandoned appearance.

I opened the glass door, and I heard the satisfying jingle of the bell as I walked in. The person at the register was tinkering with something under the counter but stood up as I entered, seemingly a little shocked to see me.

"Welcome," he said. "Let me know if you need any assistance."

I ignored him for the most part, examining the arrays of candies and chocolates in the store, but something caught the corner of my eye.

I turned to see a bag of coconut jelly beans, my favorite. I smiled as the smell of sweets wafted into my nose. Walking up to the counter, I noticed the cashier finishing one last touch on what he was working on, as a small red gem clattered to the floor.

"Umm … can I have some jelly b— no mom would kill me … but it well … uh wouldn't hurt to have … no, I really shouldn't … but uh … maybe I should then … um … can I have a bag of assorted jelly beans, please? Or maybe just coconut and not assorted … well, um … I need a minute," I exhaled.

The cashier smiled. He looked like a college student, with slightly tan skin and wavy brown hair. He wasn't fazed by my idiotic behavior at all.

"Having a bit of a problem there, right?"

"Uh, no," I said, slightly insulted.

He arched an eyebrow as if he didn't believe me.

"You're early," he commented, reaching under the desk for whatever he was crafting before.

I stared at him, slightly puzzled, as he continued.

He handed me a small, ornately decorated metal tin, his black nail polish shining in the low light. There were gold, black, and red gems on the outside, secured with a clear lid on top. On the bottom of the tin was the number *fifteen* painted in black, and inside was a small, milky white jelly bean.

It seemed like a sign of sorts. Fifteen was my favorite of all the numbers. Even though it was probably a coincidence, it still seemed like it was meant for me.

I looked up at the cashier, about to say something, when I noticed his eyes seemed to be gold-red. I blinked, and then they were back to a soft brown. I probably was dehydrated. That happened a lot in the Florida heat.

"Isn't this a jelly be—?" I asked, confused about why a single jelly bean would need such elaborate packaging.

He cut me off. "Yes, it's a jelly bean, but it's special. All your awkwardness floats away for eight perfect days. If you like it, I might give you a permanent one."

He leaned over the counter. "Hey, Ryder! How's that working for ya?"

I looked at the girl referred to as Ryder, who nodded and said, "It's going great! The stuttering's gone. It really works!"

"What does it cost?" I asked him, suspicious.

"This one's yours. You don't owe me any money," he said sweetly.

I looked back at him and the jelly bean.

"I haven't seen this place around here," I commented.

"Yeah," He nodded, a muscle in his jaw twitching. "I'm not from around here."

I was silent for a while, and then I said, "Why me?"

"You'll need it," he said flatly.

"What?" I blurted. Then added, "But when?"

"You'll know," he smiled smugly.

I stood there, and then I said, "Uh what flavor is this?"

"Coconut."

Blink.

"Sounds good!"

He nodded at me, and I went out the door. I held the jelly bean tin and looked at it for a minute. It was tempting, but my awkwardness wasn't really a problem. My friends usually accepted me.

And, seriously, eight days? Really? One day more than a week? Talk about precision problems. I was almost halfway home until I stupidly realized I hadn't actually gotten jelly beans. Well, shoot. Slightly irritated, I pulled out my house key and let myself in.

Gwen was sitting at the table, busy obsessing over her homework. I threw my backpack onto the ground with carelessness and casually placed the tin on the table.

Gwen started putting her homework away and said without looking, "Hey, Alex. How was today?"

She looked up and saw the metal tin on the table. Her face stilled before she looked up at me again, smiling tightly.

"Hey, Gwen?"

"Yeah?" she replied, her voice strained, not taking her eyes off the tin.

"I'm kinda mad at my friends."

"Well, what did they do?" Gwen finally looked up, making eye contact.

"Perry and Brit totally embarrassed me in front of Thomas," I moped.

"Well, be careful."

"What?" I asked.

"You just need to watch what you're doing sometimes. Think about your actions and the consequences before you do it, okay?" she said.

That was … random.

I took the metal tin and shoved it into my backpack. Gwen's eyes followed my hand as if I was handling a snake.

"Don't go all prophetic on me," I teased.

We both looked at each other for a long second and then broke into tense laughter.

"So, you want to play *Mario Kart* or something?" Gwen asked. "I just finished my homework …."

"Oooh, yes! Let's go!" I replied eagerly.

Gwen walked over to the large flatscreen TV and connected the Nintendo Switch to it so we could play. She finished booting it up, and we logged in.

She clicked through a few of the options, and we started selecting our characters. Gwen chose Baby Rosalina with the Mr. Scooty and button wheels. I chose Baby Daisy and just some items that I thought looked cool. Gwen liked playing strategically, whereas I didn't quite care. I just liked the coolest-looking stuff. Gwen pressed some more buttons, and we began to play.

The countdown started as I leaned forward in anticipation, pressing the 'A' button.

Gwen immediately took the lead when the game started while I was stuck behind with some NPCs.

"Oh, you're not getting away that easily!" I said, running into a mystery box as I threw a shell at Gwen's digital character.

Gwen avoided it, speeding into first place. "You can't stop me!"

"Why did you have to get so good at this game?" I groaned as a few more NPCs passed me.

"Because I wanted to beat you," Gwen chimed, accidentally getting hit by a shell. She yelped as a few NPCs sped past her.

"Uh oh! Guess you're not so high and mighty now, eh?" I grinned, taking second place.

I passed the finish line as I began the next round. I only trash-talked with Gwen. I could never act like this with my friends.

"Alright, bet," Gwen said, holding second place.

"Nope. I'm not losing money to you again," I said.

Gwen laughed. "Oh, come on! I want five dollars so I can buy ice cream or something,"

"Well, buy it yourself!" I retaliated, trying to focus on the laps.

"I will! With your money!"

"I'm not betting on this."

It was quiet for a few seconds as I continued in the lead.

"Alright, I'll bet you five dollars I'm going to win."

"Yes!" Gwen cheered. "You finally gave in!"

"Well, guess what? You're not getting my—"

Gwen did some crazy move and passed me, winning the round.

"Arrgh," I groaned. "Not again."

"Ha. You don't really have to pay me. We still have some ice cream in the fridge."

"Aww, thanks!" I said.

"Didn't say you were getting any," Gwen said playfully.

"Hey!"

"Want to play again?" she asked.

"Yes, but I need to work on my essay. I'll get some of it done, and maybe we can play after dinner," I said, grabbing my backpack and heading down the hall to my room.

I started pulling items out of my backpack, placing the tin on my desk. I turned my phone off to focus, so I wouldn't be distracted. I pulled up my laptop and logged into Canvas for the assignment details.

I glanced at the small ornate tin.

I had a feeling that taking the tin was a bad idea and that I should give it back. It was stupid getting it in the first place. The shop was kind of sketchy, and the tin looked expensive. Maybe the tin cost a bunch, and he would report it as stolen? Did the jelly bean actually taste like coconut? Eight days? Why did I believe that guy?

I shoved the tin into my backpack with a plan to drop it off tomorrow. Yes, the sooner I had it out of my hands, the better.

CHAPTER TWO – WEDNESDAY

I yawned, my hand fluttering to my mouth as spots began to clear from my eyes.

"You good?"

"Huh?" I asked groggily, noticing Gwen brushing her hair in the bathroom.

I yawned again, struggling to move my knotty hair out of my face.

"You need help with that?" she asked as I walked up to the sink, grabbing my toothbrush.

I nodded slowly, glancing at her. She looked fine, but I did not. My hair was a wild mess, and I felt more or less like absolute crap. Even the foggy mirror could show that.

"Did you get any sleep?" she asked, beginning to run the brush through my hair.

I accidentally stopped paying attention. Where did she get the brush from?

"Um," I started, rubbing my eyes. I felt a tug in my hair, but it didn't bother me. "I think I got maybe like four or five hours?"

"That's painfully relatable," she sighed, untangling a knot. "So why were you staying up so late?"

"There was an essay," I said.

Gwen laughed a little. "You've never stayed up that late for an essay before."

"I also had to reread Natalie's fanfic chapter. I looked like an idiot yesterday when I forgot."

"How long was that chapter?" Gwen asked, smirking a little.

"Uhhh, ten thousand words or something?"

Gwen raised her eyebrows, smacking her lips. "That's not a chapter. That's a book."

"Eh, she's crazy," I laughed.

Gwen put down the brush. My hair actually looked half decent. I ran my hand through, and like a miracle, it didn't get caught.

"Hey, when are you going to finish your Bat Mitzvah speech?" Gwen asked as I began to leave the room.

"I don't know," I sighed. "I just can't think of anything. And it's boring and confusing."

"Well, you'll figure something out," Gwen smiled slightly.

Doubtful. My Bat mitzvah speech was coming up soon, and with that, my Bat Mitzvah. The speech was always the difficult part after the whole 'learning a new language' thing. Because not only did I have to learn the Torah portion and haftarah, I had to also write a speech about how that connected to my daily life. Precisely my conundrum.

"Also, thanks for brushing my hair," I said. "I probably should get dressed."

"Yeah," Gwen said. "You do that. And try not to stay up so late again."

"Alright!" I said, closing the door of my room.

I grabbed an orange dry-fit and a pair of black shorts. Sure, it was Halloween colors, and it might have been a month too late, but I always prioritized comfort over looks. Luckily the conversation with Gwen had woken me up. Well, maybe not entirely, but still. I opened the door, quickly making my lunch and finishing the rest of my morning routine.

"Bye," I said, beginning to close the door. "Lock it, please."

Gwen gave me a small wave, and the lock clicked behind me.

The cold slammed into me as I stepped outside, and I shivered as I walked past the shrubbery spilling into the concrete walkway. Pulling up my backpack, I strode across the sidewalk. After a few minutes, I reached the fence, reaching out my fingers as they shook slightly.

"Hey, girl!" Someone chimed, turning around.

The girl's slick ponytail flipped around, her dark brown and light gold hair settling on her shoulders. This was punishment for sleeping in.

"Hi, Brit," I said weakly, walking forward as Perry and Brit stopped.

Brit's face lit up. She seemed so back and forth all the time. Sometimes she was stupid, rude, or weirdly nice. And this time, she was the latter.

"So …" Perry started, her eyes glinting.

Her black hair rustled in the wind a little, revealing a mischievous grin on her face.

"So what?" I asked, confused.

Brit tucked a strand of her hair back into her ponytail, grinning stupidly at me.

"How's it going with you-know-who?" Brit pressed.

I went blank.

"Who?" I asked.

I obviously looked like an idiot, but I legitimately didn't know.

"Thomas!" Perry giggled, glancing at Brit.

The latter was still smiling obnoxiously and let out an overly loud laugh.

"Um, I don't know what you mean," I said, glancing at the two of them. "We're not a thing. I mean, of course, we're not; he barely knows I exist.

I don't even really like him," I stuttered, my face going hot. "I mean, I like him but as a friend! Not as that y'know, um, we're just friends and um—"

I had begun sweating, my cheeks hotter than ever as I rambled.

"Oh, come on, bestie! It's so obvious that you like him!" Brit squealed.

I blinked. "Um, don't call me bestie? We're … not that close."

"Fine," Brit said, a sharp edge to her tone. "How's science going?"

I exhaled in exasperation. I just couldn't deal with them. Brit knew I hated science, and she wouldn't shut up about it for that exact reason. Neither would Perry. I rolled my eyes in a playful way so they wouldn't notice my irritation. I walked faster so I could leave them behind, gritting my teeth once they couldn't see me.

Once at the school, I made my way through the halls to the library. The familiar smell of musty books flooded in. I sat at the normal table where everyone was sitting except for Perry and Brit, who had luckily stopped at their lockers.

"So, uh … what are you guys talking about?" I asked as the room quieted down a bit.

"*Animal Crossing*," Thomas said. "Talking about what we have in our villages and stuff."

"Oh, uh … thanks," I said awkwardly as I sat down.

"Alright, so I have a blue rose," Natalie began, as I almost immediately cut her off.

"You have a *blue rose*!" I exclaimed.

"Shhhhhhhh!" They all hissed.

"What? I'm not loud," I replied.

"You are, but that's not a huge problem. Just be a little quieter," Natalie said gently.

I got a lump in my throat hearing that as they continued talking. I knew she wasn't trying to hurt my feelings, but it didn't make me feel too great, nevertheless.

The library door creaked open, and Perry and Brit stepped inside. They found their way into the conversation with ease. Why was it so simple for them?

"So, who's everyone sitting next to in reading?" Angel asked. "We all got a seating change, right?"

I nodded. "Yep. Sitting next to Perry and Brit now."

"It's pretty nice," Brit commented.

"You're so lucky," Natalie said. "At least you guys get to sit next to who you like. I have to sit next to Josh."

"I'm sorry," Angel said. "He's so … gross."

"Agreed," Thomas said.

A few others nodded their heads.

"I'm sitting next to Ava," Angel complained. "I have her number now, and she's texting me nonstop."

"Ava gave you her number? That's insane," Natalie said.

Angel added, "And she's liking my *Instagram* posts from last week."

"That's definitely weird," Thomas replied.

"That is weird, but if she's bothering you, then just block her," I said.

"Then she'll suspect something and confront me about it," Angel said.

"You could always request a seat change," Thomas replied.

"But she could always send *The Pops* after me," Angel insisted, her cheeks beginning to redden. "Or worse, post about me on *Insta*."

"True," I replied.

The Pops held grudges, and they got revenge on people. Time and time again, I had seen them harassing another person on social media who did them wrong. I didn't want to admit it, but if Angel removed contact with Ava, things wouldn't be pretty.

"I'm sorry you're stuck with her. Any idea why she keeps texting you? Maybe she needs help in the class?" I offered.

Angel opened her mouth to speak but was interrupted by the homeroom bell.

We walked to homeroom a few minutes later, not paying attention to the school news playing in the background. After some light conversation, the bell rang, and I made my way to first period.

I stopped by my locker, attempting to open the red door. As usual, I put in my locker combination, but it wouldn't open. I lightly tugged on it. It didn't move. I pulled harder. Still didn't move. Why must objects hate me?

I was about ready to find the nearest sledgehammer when I felt a hand on my shoulder and jumped in surprise.

"Thomas!" I exclaimed, my eyes going wide.

Did he just see me being stupid? Maybe a portal would open, and I could fall through.

"Um, are you okay?" Thomas asked.

"Yeah, I just can't get my locker open," I said, trying again and failing miserably.

Thomas grabbed the lock, quickly twisting the knob and opening the locker with ease. "There you go," he said.

"... how did you know my combination?"

"Well, you use the same combination at camp every year, so I've seen it once or twice," he grinned. "Angel also knows it, but we decided not to tell Natalie because she definitely wants to find your fanart folder."

"I guess that's a wise decision," I laughed, grabbing my books. "So, um, thanks for that."

"Yeah," he said. "Not a problem. See you."

"Bye!" I called as he walked down the hall.

I finished using my locker and rushed to Mrs. Esma's class. I sat down at my usual seat in a table group with a few people I didn't really know.

Thomas knew my locker combination. He took the time to remember it? Did that mean he was noticing me? Although Angel knew it also, so maybe it was just a friend thing.

Mrs. Esma cleared her throat. "Alright, everyone. Before we start, please pull out your binders and papers." She turned to me. "Alex."

I blinked, looking back at Mrs. Esma in a panic after realizing I hadn't pulled out my binders or pencils.

"Oh, I'm … I'm sorry," I said, hurriedly pulling out my supplies.

I grimaced a bit as other people in the class glanced at me. I located my assignment and handed it to her. She moved on after a few seconds, talking about the homework from the previous night.

"Today, we will be starting a new project," Mrs. Esma announced, flipping on a presentation. "To show that you understand the concept of our last unit, your groups will be designing a fictional society to show how civilizations are formed. I need one person from your table group to come here and collect a rule sheet."

There were a few quiet groans from the announcement of a project. One person at our table stood up to grab the papers and passed a sheet to me and the others.

"So, as you might have guessed, this is a group project. Four people per group. And don't worry about finishing it today; it's due in three weeks, so that you don't have to work over *The Week*, but you can if you want to."

Charlene raised her hand quickly as Mrs. Esma called on her. "Can we choose who we work with?"

"No. I've already picked your groups. The requirements for this project are simple, as you'll see on your paper …"

Mrs. Esma continued talking as I zoned out. It was a good thing I had a directions sheet, or else I would be incredibly lost.

"When you get your group assignment, move to another table to begin working," Mrs. Esma said.

I glanced at Natalie, Thomas, and Angel from across the room, and then *The Pops* nervously glanced at each other from the corner of my eye. I desperately wanted to stay in my group, but there wasn't a high chance I would get exactly who I wanted.

"To start off, we have Mallory, Charlene, Thomas, and Angel in group one," Mrs. Esma said.

Charlene immediately groaned, and Angel and Thomas made irritated looks toward her.

"Our second group is Natalie, Ava, Nina, and Alex."

I shared a glance with Natalie for a second as Mrs. Esma continued calling out names. My group walked over to an empty desk. I wasn't thrilled to be working with any of *The Pops*, but at least it wasn't Charlene.

It was quiet for a few seconds before Natalie spoke up.

"So, what is this project exactly?" Natalie asked, glancing at Ava and Nina from across the table.

"Mrs. Esma said we were supposed to create a society, so um … hold on, just let me look at the rules," Ava said, glancing over at the sheet.

"Okay, so we need to make rules, but before we do that shouldn't we split up rol—" I started.

"Ah! Okay, here it is; we have to make ten rules," Ava pointed to the paper. "Basically, laws and the sort. Somebody should look at the Constitution for reference to figure out what we should have in there," Ava said, her eyes glued to the paper.

"That makes sense. But like Alex said, we probably should split up the roles just to see how much work everyone's going to do. If everyone's alright with it, I could probably take the majority of the work," Natalie said.

"Oh, um, yeah I guess I'm alright with that," I said.

I didn't want to say that I really wanted to do some parts of the project, but it was clear Natalie didn't trust *The Pops* enough to pull their weight.

"I don't think you should take the majority." Ava pouted. "We should probably share it equally? Like based off of slide numbers or different tasks, like someone does design and research, and another person compiles it. Then there could be a presenter. Wait … do we all present or just one person?"

"I'm not exactly sure about the presentation rules, but that works," Natalie said.

"Yeah! Or we could have two people do design, or one person does design, and two people do research. And maybe someone could be a fact checker?" Ava said.

Nina looked up from her phone. I hadn't exactly noticed she was texting or that she was even there at all.

"Could we just get this over with? And I want the design role; I don't feel like doing anything else," she groaned, only sort of paying attention. She glanced at her phone, mumbling. "Oh my gosh, why did he say that?"

I rolled my eyes. "Okay then, so I think that's good. We have some pretty good ideas but one of the things it says—"

Nina cut me off. "Oh my god, he did *not* just send me that. Ava, look at this!" she said, showing it to Ava.

"Um, Nina, we're supposed to be working on the project," Ava said politely. "You have to get an *A* otherwise, you can't see him. Remember last week?"

"Yeah, I know, but like—" Nina tried.

"Okay, guys, could we go back to work? Alex was talking," Natalie said.

This was going to be quite the project.

Ava grabbed Nina's phone, putting it face down on the table. "Yeah, yeah. We're focused, right, Nina?" she said, glaring at her for a second.

Nina leaned back in her seat, crossing her arms over her chest. "Yeah, whatever," she sighed.

"So, what I was saying was we should probably figure out what type of government we should have? Like a democracy, or a monarchy or something like that," I said. "I don't exactly know; what do you guys think?"

"Can't we just do communism?" Nina asked. "That'd be more fun."

"Okay, although that would be funny, I don't know if we would get a good grade. Also, communism is more economy-based, and we're talking about rulers," Natalie explained.

"Ugh, whatever." Nina sighed

Ava nudged Nina in the arm with her elbow. "Nina. We have to do this project. Just focus."

They stared at each other for a long minute. I held my breath, not daring to look away. It was like two lions facing each other down.

Finally, Nina exhaled and said *fine* in a way that meant that things were not fine.

Ava looked back at Natalie and me. "Well, I don't know. I think all the other groups would probably choose democracy. Y'know, for obvious reasons. But we shouldn't really do that because there's more competition if more people are doing it. Maybe we should have a constitutional monarchy? Either that or we could do a more socialist type of perspective. I don't think anyone would do that," Ava said.

"That's a good idea," Natalie chirped. "I definitely don't think we should choose democracy. From a perspective of what Mrs. Esma likes more, we could get creative and do an oligarchy where we split up the land between fictional rulers," she added.

Ava's face lit up. "Ooh! If we're doing oligarchy, we could go from the beginning of Rome's structure with Romulus and Remus. Like two rulers heading an oligarchy. Maybe that could qualify as an oligarchy? We could start research there," Ava said.

"Wait, what do you mean? Beginning of Rome?" I asked.

Nina leaned forward. "Well, Rome was first started by two brothers, Romulus and Remus. They ruled together for a bit until a bit of murder and betrayal happened. We could mimic the plan Romulus and Remus had to set up Rome as our oligarchy model because there isn't really an oligarchy that's just two people."

My mouth popped open. This was the most I had heard Nina speak in any class. Ava and Natalie also had their mouths agape.

"What?" Nina spat, looking at each of us.

I blinked and recovered first. "Oh! That's a pretty good idea. So how would we know it wouldn't get too corrupt?" I asked.

"Well, it's a fake society for a reason, right?" Ava chuckled.

"Sorry, I wasn't paying attention earlier. I don't know if we talked about the roles yet, but could I take design? And Ava should definitely take research. Who wants to take the management job?" Nina asked.

"I could take managing," Natalie said. "I think I could work pretty well with Ava, so if that's alright with you all, it's alright with me."

"So, should we make a group chat? I don't know, this project's due in like three weeks, and it'll be hard to communicate and stuff," Nina said.

"I think I have your numbers from the mass group chat, but I could probably check later," I replied.

"Just put in your numbers here," Nina said, handing us her phone with an empty text screen. "Does anyone have an Android?"

"No, we don't have Androids," Natalie said, putting in her number.

"Oh good, I hate it when the stupid text bubbles are green," Nina mumbled, grabbing the phone after we finished putting in our numbers. "Oh my god, why is he texting me that? My mom literally looks through my phone. I'm going to have to delete this stuff."

Nina looked up from her phone. "Oh, you guys can keep talking."

"Um, yeah," I said. "Okay, so we have most things in order. When do you all want to meet?"

"Sometime after school next week. Nina, do you think you could have some sketches by then? I think it would be cool if we could have some illustrations of our city because I don't think anyone else is going to draw it," Ava said.

"Oh, dude, yeah, I'd be down. As long as we have a flower thing because they're so cool to draw. If we could have a botanical garden or a field in the city, that'd be great. Honestly, I'd love to do that," Nina said.

"Alright, you guys okay with a botanical garden in a city?" Ava asked.

"That sounds nice. Nina, do you think you could draw a map or something? Because that'd be really cool, but you don't have to. I have this app that can make maps easily," I said.

"Oh, I probably have the same app. What's it called?" she asked curiously, opening her phone to see if she could find it.

"*Worldbox*. Do you have it?" I asked.

"Yeah! I use that app to base my other maps off of. Like, I start the world and do a couple edits so I can make it like a really cool beginning of a book-style map. Y'know, like *The Hobbit*?" Nina said.

"I do that too! Sometimes I make maps to give to Natalie over here because she likes to write stuff a lot, so that's pretty cool." I smiled to myself. The thought that Nina and I bonded was quite the achievement for someone like me. "So, next week's good for me. We can probably figure out the date in the group chat."

"Yeah. I'm good every day except for … hmm. I'd have to check with Red because I know we scheduled a date, but I don't know what day," Nina said. "I'll text you what day I'm available."

"I'm good for any day, really," Ava said.

"Same. Any day except Monday, though, because Mondays are already really stressful," Natalie said.

"I think that's good. We have like three minutes until the end of class. We should probably start packing up, right?"

Nina looked at her phone. "Yeah, we probably— He sent 57 messages. Are you kidding? He's actually crazy …." Nina said, getting up.

"Text you in the group chat!" Ava called.

"Alright!" I replied, walking back to my seat with Natalie. "And I guess we're going to be texting with Ava also."

"At least Angel won't be alone. I expected this to be far worse," Natalie said. "I'm glad Nina was only texting for half the meeting."

"Yeah," I said. "So, I'll see you at lunch."

"Bye," Natalie said, walking off.

Reading rushed by, and soon it was time for math. I reached for the handle. Algebra was calling my name. I could feel the beautiful numbers that would start pouring from my mouth. I just had to open the door and get through the next few days, and then I could hang out with Jay and Raaj on the weekend.

But before I could do any of that, I heard a voice.

"That outfit is hideous. Do you not own a mirror? I can't even stand to be in the same hallway as you."

I covered my face with my hands a bit. I could tell from the voice it was Charlene. Wearing orange and black together was such a big mistake.

I inhaled, steeling myself as I turned around. But the venom wasn't directed at me, to my surprise. Charlene and Mallory were spitting their words at a sixth-grade girl who I recognized since we were in band camp last summer before I decided to quit. She was clutching her instrument case as if it could protect her from Charlene's rapid-fire insults. What was her name? Madonna? Moxie? It didn't matter. I turned back to the classroom door; it wasn't my fight.

I heard more vicious laughter from behind me and sobs from the girl. Before I knew what I was doing, my feet turned, and my mouth opened.

"Hey!" I yelled. "Leave her alone!"

Hmmm … Natalie was right. I *was* loud.

I caught their attention. Oh, sh—what was I thinking?

Everything began to move in slow motion. Charlene and Mallory slowly turned to face me, as did several bystanders in the hallway.

"What?" Mallory asked coldly, her eyes narrowing.

The sixth-grade girl dashed away. Oh, how I wished I was her.

"I-I …" My mouth went dry.

Charlene rolled her eyes as she took in my outfit.

"What did you say, *Pumpkin?*"

I gritted my teeth as I felt a fire inside of me.

"Why do you think you guys can do whatever you want? You don't have a special privilege or some stupid trait about you that makes you special. So, stop taking it out on other people because it doesn't make you any better. It just makes you worse. If you're scared you'll lose your popularity, then stop being a jerk to whoever you come up to!" I snapped.

There was a pause, and I could see something resembling surprise flicker on Mallory's face as she glanced at Charlene.

"And who do you think you are?" Charlene hissed.

"I—" I started.

She scoffed in response.

"That's what I thought," she spat, a smile curling on her lips as she whipped around.

The crowd in the hallway dissipated, and the confrontation came to a close.

I was frozen. The few people who were watching left. I finally turned and opened the door to math, which I was luckily on time for. At least I could escape *them* for a while.

The feelings of stress flew by quick as soon as I solved the daily math question.

"Alright, class. Now it's time to review our question. Anyone have the answer?" Mr. Koffman asked.

It was a very complex algebraic equation. No one had their hand raised except for me.

"Alex."

"Twenty-seven," I said, without even the slightest hesitation.

"Whoa. How'd you do that so fast? You really should be on the math team," Raaj commented.

"I could show you if you want," I offered.

"Great idea, Alex. Why don't we all split up into groups and give tips on how to solve them," Mr. Koffman said.

Normally people hated groups, but most people didn't seem to mind when it was to share tips.

The room erupted into the sounds of scraping chairs across the hard tile floor. I joined Raaj and Jay at the table. They were the best players on the team, that much I knew.

Mr. Koffman gave us our problem to solve. Linear equations. Piece of cake.

We all solved it individually, and then it was time to share our techniques.

"I got forty-five," I said.

"I got that, too," Jay agreed.

Raaj nodded his head.

"But how do you do it so fast? Just to answer my question," Raaj said.

"Can I see your math really quickly?" I asked.

He handed me his paper.

"Whoa. I've never seen anyone do it this way before. It might take longer, but it's still right," I said.

"So how do you do it?" he asked.

"I just take a shortcut right there, and then all you have to do is multiply that."

He grinned. "Thank you so much. I never knew that."

"So again … how come you aren't on our math team?" Jay asked.

I didn't want to mention I was too nervous to audition.

"I really wanted to sign up, but I couldn't get a spot in time," I fibbed. It was half true, at least.

"You're gonna get a spot next year; that's guaranteed. And maybe there is room this year to be an alternate."

"Really?" I asked.

Jay said, "Talk to Mr. Koffman. Another alternate wouldn't hurt, and then you'll know what to expect for next year."

I just smiled, more to myself. I was a little distracted thinking about going with the team to events and the rush of solving equations. Maybe next year would be better.

.   .   .

The sidewalk was quiet, and a few patches of leaves covered me from the afternoon sun. The candy shop was still nestled on its corner, the lights turned out, and the establishment empty.

I took off my backpack for a second, checking to see if the jelly bean was there. It was still in the front pocket. I sighed, walking home. I guessed I'd return it tomorrow. It took a few minutes until the candy shop was out of view, and I was standing at the door of my house, walking inside.

Gwen was out, and I decided to ignore my homework for a few hours. I got on my phone and pulled up *FaceTime* on the group chat, sitting in my chair.

"Hey, guys!" I said, waving at the phone screen as I turned on my computer.

"Hey!" Angel replied, loading into the call.

"Guess what!" Brit said excitedly, her voice slightly muffled by static.

"Yeah?" Thomas asked.

"I got a 100% on that reading test last week!"

I wasn't really good at reading; I only got an 80%.

"Hey! Good job!" I said.

Brit blushed pridefully.

"So …" Natalie started. "I got an inspiration burst, and I finished the next three chapters of my fanfic!"

"No way!" Angel exclaimed. "It took you four weeks to finish the last one!"

"Alright, guys I'm logging into the server," I said, clicking on the *Minecraft* icon.

"I'm getting on as well," Thomas replied.

The screen loaded as I logged onto the server. After a few seconds, I spawned in my base in front of my red-colored bed. I was notified that more people logged on.

"We're in," Angel said. "I just want you all to know that I'll be setting up a server-wide game soon if I can get a few more materials for my build. So does anyone have obsidian?"

I opened my inventory and shared what I had. I might not have been popular, or smart, or talented, but I had my friends, and that was enough.

CHAPTER THREE – THURSDAY

I climbed out of my bed and yawned. I could smell the delightful aroma of fresh, buttery pancakes with butterscotch and chocolate chips. Luckily, Gwen knew enough to cook and not set the house on fire. It was something Mom taught her a few years ago during the pandemic. We were both homeschooled that year, and our parents went out of their way to do extra things with us. We learned cooking skills, read classic literature, and watched a bunch of 80's movies. I was glad we had vaccines and that I was able to go to school, but at times I missed the slowness.

I came into the kitchen and could tell that Mom and Dad had already left for the day. I grabbed one of our white ceramic plates and piled on the pancakes.

"MmmmMMmmMm. Theessse are sooo guuud," I said, pancakes still crammed into my mouth.

They were delicious and soft, and the bursts of smooth chocolate throughout the pancake added an extra sweet and buttery flavor.

Gwen chuckled. "I'm glad. I have to leave early, so I'm heading out now. Make sure you lock the door."

I decided to head out shortly after Gwen left. I opened the door, and the cold found its way through my thin, pink shirt and tickled my bones. I hated Florida for that. Why couldn't it just have nice weather? Why did it always have to be damp-cold or stupid-hot?

I caught sight of the sunrise. It was a red sky, so the seas would probably be rough or something. But it wasn't really my problem, so I settled with taking in the beauty of the sunrise.

"Hey Alex!" Natalie called from behind me.

I turned around to see Natalie and Thomas smiling as they caught up to me.

After our gaming session yesterday, it was hard to stop talking about *Minecraft*.

"So …" I started, walking in between the two of them. "Do you have any spare Netherite in the school server?"

"I do," Natalie said. "Just visit my base after school, and I'll be glad to give you some."

"Thanks! You're a lifesaver," I said. "I really needed a pickaxe because mine broke, and I had to get gold really quickly because insta-mining is really satisfying." I blew into my hands since they were starting to feel numb at the tips. "And I forgot to enchant, and do you have mending books because they really help, and it's totally okay if you don—"

"Alex, pause. You're like talking a lot," Thomas quipped.

My face turned red. "I *am?*"

He shook his head. "It's cool, Alex. We all talk a lot," he said. "I just wanted to tell you I have mending books."

"Really?" I asked. "Thanks."

He nodded. "Nat, I could probably give you some if you needed it as well."

"Oh my god, thank you," Natalie sighed in relief. "You're a lifesaver."

Angel caught up to us at the library. I felt so lucky to have known them for so many years. I met Natalie before we even began school. It was the first day of kindergarten. She was across the room, huddling behind her Mom. After a bit of considering, I nervously introduced myself, stumbling over every other word. Although it was a shaky introduction, the rest was history. We were at the assigned snack table with Angel and Thomas. Apparently, fruit snacks had sealed the deal. In second grade, we did our own *blood oath* in a circle around the oak tree. We sliced up the fruit gummies, mashed them together between our joined palms, and then ate them. It had been the four of us for the past several years.

"Hey!" Angel said, striding into the room, sitting down at a chair.

Some people in the group responded with *hellos* as we took our seats.

"So, how is everyone?" I asked, glancing around.

"Fine," Perry said. "But you don't need to be so annoying."

"I literally just said hello," I argued, glancing at the others.

They seemed to be taken aback by Perry's attitude but didn't say anything.

"Well yeah, but some people here just want some peace and quiet, and you kind of mess that up," Perry snapped.

I felt my stomach sink as I closed my mouth.

Angel glanced at me to say something but stopped when she realized Perry would probably snap at her as well.

After a few minutes, Thomas spoke up, and the tension in the air lessened. It was easier to talk without Perry's bad mood hanging over the room, but it didn't change the fact I still felt dread looming in my stomach after the stinging comment.

"What's going on in your project?" Natalie asked. "You got in the group with Mallory and Charlene, right?"

Thomas nodded. "Yeah. Mallory's trying to cut Angel and me out of the whole project and just do everything herself."

"And Charlene just won't stop texting and actually pay attention,"

Angel said. "What's going on with you guys?"

"Surprisingly, Ava's making an effort to help," Natalie said. "She's actually giving some pretty decent advice. Nina's mainly texting Red, but she's still helpful."

"Yeah," I said. "Ava is giving good advice."

"Alex, I just said that," Natalie said playfully.

I turned red. "You *did*?"

"Yeah," Angel chuckled. "But it's alright."

"Okay," I said, trying not to sweat from embarrassment as the conversation continued.

When the bell rang, Angel and I walked slower than the others to talk, hoping to get some quick privacy.

"Hello? Perry was so rude!" I exclaimed, crossing my arms.

"She really was," Angel said. "I'll talk to her. I don't know what's gotten into her, but I'll fix it."

I didn't have the courage to say that Perry was always like this to me when we were alone. What if everyone thought that about me, but they didn't say anything like Perry? What if everyone thought I was annoying? What if Thomas thought I was annoying?

I interrupted my thoughts, complaining to Angel before I could spiral more.

"Thanks. She just … ugh! I can't deal with her all the time," I grumbled.

"That's fine," Angel said. "I'll handle this, k?"

"Yeah," I sighed.

It was quiet for a few seconds.

"Angel," I started. "Am I … annoying?"

"No! Of course not!" Angel exclaimed. "Perry's just being rude. We adore you!"

"Okay," I said, feeling a bit better.

But I wasn't sure if I really believed it.

.   .   .

I entered the door and solved the math problem in a heartbeat. I got it right, as usual. The normal praise was acquired, and halfway through class, Mr. Koffman announced we would be holding a mock math competition. I joined Raaj's team at their table, and on the opposite end, Jay was leading the other team.

"First question," Mr. Koffman said.

The question flashed on the smart board. We all started solving the problem until we heard the buzzer.

"Jay's team, you may answer first."

"Ninety-two," Jay said.

Raaj glanced down at my paper and saw that my answer was different. He grinned, knowing we had gotten it right.

"I'm sorry that is incorrect," Mr. Koffman said.

Jay sighed, but I called across the table. "It was just a single problem. No one's gonna get everything right. This is how we all get better."

Normally, when someone said something that cheesy, whoever said it would probably be made fun of. Jay was different. He gave me a thumbs-up.

The next item flashed on the smart board.

I put my head down and started to work on the equation. I finished and lifted my head to see the others still scribbling. The buzzer went off.

"Raaj's team, what is your answer?"

Raaj opened his mouth to give his response but then noticed the circled answer on my paper. I had time to do it twice, getting the same answer. I looked at Raaj, and his calculation was different from mine.

"Raaj, what is your reply?" Mr. Koffman asked.

Raaj's eyes lifted, making contact with mine. He reached over and pulled my paper close to him, saying, "Negative five x minus one to the second power, over seven."

"Where are your parentheses?"

Raaj cleared his throat. "Parentheses outside of the negative five x minus one. The parentheses unit is to the second power." He continued to look at me. I waited, suddenly doubting myself.

"Good job, Raaj."

The class broke into applause. Raaj shook his head. I heard him say

"Damn seventh grader" under his breath before he looked up, grinning at me. He mouthed *Saturday* before picking up his pencil for the next problem. My cheeks flushed, and I put my head down to work.

.   .   .

PE was an evil sandwich of popular parasites.

And also the biggest regret of my life.

I went into the locker rooms to change. The popular girls always took the section with the good benches. I looked over at them, irritated. I pulled off my dark blue dry-fit shorts and made the rookie mistake of sitting on a broken bench to change. With no delay, the bench failed on me, and I slid to the opposite side, onto the ground. Without hesitation, snickering filled the room. I quickly changed into my ugly, gray gym uniform as I evil-eyed the popular girls. I rolled my eyes as they brushed their hair and added a new layer of fresh lipstick. To exercise. It was revolting. It was gonna get ruined anyway, so I didn't know why they even bothered.

I weaved my way through the locker room and into the expansive gym. I walked to the center of the room, where others were doing stretches.

"Josh, go ahead and grab the dodgeball bag," Coach Hill said.

Whoever invented dodgeball was an evil mastermind, but at least I was decent at dodging. When the game started, I was doing much better than I normally did.

"Red, Perry. You are both out," Coach yelled.

I continued to avoid the ball but almost collided with someone.

"Watch it, A," a boy from my reading class said.

"Oops. Sorry!" I called out, moving quickly.

Did he just call me A? Like, as in a nickname? I smiled a little to myself.

Around halfway through the game, I heard a thud and a wail. I turned around and saw a person crumpled on the ground, holding their bloody nose as an orange ball rolled away from them. Coach told us he had to take them to the nurse's office and said we had to stop the game in case someone else got hurt. He said he would call another teacher to come in and supervise. When they left, we all stood around and looked at each other, unsure what to do.

"Guys!" Charlene's voice rang out across the room, calling everyone to her attention.

It worked way better than the teacher's method because, unlike the teachers, she could socially ruin your reputation for something like not shutting up.

"Let's play *Truth or Dare*," she said.

Everyone nodded in agreement, but I could tell most of the students were uncomfortable. They weren't making eye contact and were unusually quiet. Charlene motioned for us to gather in a circle on the floor of the gym. I tried to make myself as small as possible, as did many others. I settled on the cold wooden floor as Charlene chose Perry and Brit to pick the people.

"Josh, *Truth or Dare*?" Perry said.

"Dare," he said confidently. He was the captain of the basketball team, so there wasn't any real risk involved for him.

Perry and Brit talked quietly with Charlene, and then Brit announced, "Do a handstand for two minutes."

He grinned and got up to comply.

Perry added, "While reciting Romeo's balcony scene."

Brit giggled a little. Josh groaned as people pulled out their phones to record him.

While upside down, Josh began, "Wherefore out thy …"

Some of the girls around us began to giggle when his t-shirt fell over his face, but he continued to recite what he could remember.

After he finished, Perry and Brit continued selecting.

"Alex." I heard Perry sneer.

No … no, no, no. Why me?

I looked up, making eye contact with Perry.

"*Truth or Dare*?" she said, her face pinching.

I inhaled. "Dare."

Why did I say that? Dares terrified me, and I'd rather just be honest instead of doing something stupid.

Perry and Brit whispered to Charlene.

Perry turned triumphantly towards me, placing her hand on her hip. "Tell Thomas you hate him after class," she said, her lips forming into a smirk.

My face fell. I started to feel my heart race, and … was that sweat running down my back? I *really liked* him. I tried to imagine Thomas' face and saying those words to his sweet brown eyes.

"No way," I said, rolling my eyes.

My hand reached into my pocket, feeling the gems along the side of the jelly bean tin. Maybe it could fix this. But being awkward wasn't the issue at the moment.

Perry's face pinched tighter, and her eyes narrowed before she took a step toward me. "You have to."

She glanced over at Charlene, who was watching us curiously now.

Perry continued, "That's how the game works. You. Can't. Say. No."

I jumped to my feet. "No!" I shouted.

I was done with Perry and her manipulation. Being rude, making fun of me, calling me annoying, and now this. I was done with it. My feet walked towards her, forcing me to follow. I was almost nose-to-nose with her.

"I won't tell Thomas that! But you—you clearly aren't a friend. I hate you!" To my relief, the bell rang right after those words came out of my mouth. Everyone walked away, but Perry and I stood there locked in a stare-down.

Eventually, Brit said, "Let's go, Perry. I don't want to be late."

They both walked off, and Charlene was standing at the edge of the gym, eyeing me before going into the locker room again.

I sighed and could feel my limbs start to shake with exhaustion. I heard the bell ring. This was going to be another day that I just wore my gym clothes to writing class.

.   .   .

I threw my backpack at the floor before stomping into the living room.

"Hey, what happened?" Gwen asked, putting down her phone.

"Just had an awful day," I grumbled. "My friends were being so mean."

"Do you want to talk about it?" Gwen asked.

"No," I said, sighing. "I just want to calm down or something."

"Well, Mom made food last night," Gwen said. "You wanna watch *Into the Spider-Verse* over lasagna or something?"

"Sounds good to me," I said.

"I'll go heat it up. You breathe and get the movie started," she said as she walked into the kitchen.

I kept thinking about earlier in the day. What the hell was wrong with Perry? She clearly was trying to ruin my friendship with Thomas. Would she try to ruin my friendship with Angel? But she would never leave me. Should I have talked to Angel and told her what Perry did in gym class?

"It's hot," Gwen said, handing me a plate and interrupting my thoughts.

I pressed *play* on the remote.

An animated character in a bright red suit rushed across the screen.

"My name is Peter Parker. I was bitten by a radioactive spider …" I heard Gwen say to herself.

I sat my plate down on the coffee table and leaned my head on Gwen's shoulder. She put her arm around me as we continued watching.

Miles Morales began walking down the street to school. On cue, he tripped on his own shoelace as his dad's police car parked in front of him.

"'You gotta say I love you back,'" Gwen quoted in sync with the movie.

"Nooo, the embarrassment!" I said, laughing with Gwen.

"I swear high school isn't like this," Gwen said, referencing the rude comments Miles received when he walked into school.

"I hope not," I laughed, grabbing my garlic toast and starting to chew loudly. "How can he be so awkward but make it look cool?"

"Some people think he's weird. But he has some people who are his friends." She popped the last piece of bread into her mouth. "Everyone won't like you. But you do need to have someone. You can't go it alone. Even Miles and Peter need help from others."

I leaned back into Gwen. "Sometimes I feel really alone."

Gwen started to stroke my hair. "I'm always here for you."

"I wish you went to my school. It would make it so much easier." I sniffled.

Gwen continued to hold me. "I know, Alex. It won't always be this hard. Some days just have big emotions. Was there anything that was good about today?" she asked.

Math, I thought.

It was always Math. There was always an answer, always certain that you would be right or wrong.

And the idea of being an alternate lingered in my head too.

.   .   .

I glanced at my phone again before plugging it into the wall. I texted Angel after the movie and again before brushing my teeth. Sometimes she turned her phone off, especially if she had a lot of practice. Band tended to limit how much time she had to text. Even so, I really wanted to talk to her and share what Perry did. I assumed I'd tell Angel and Thomas the next day.

They trusted me, and if they knew Perry was acting like that, they definitely wouldn't be happy. I took a deep breath. I would solve everything tomorrow. It was just one big misunderstanding. I wouldn't need the jelly bean or anything like that, I was fine without it, and there would be no circumstance I would ever need it. I could handle this myself.

I slept better that night than I had in quite a while.

CHAPTER FOUR – FRIDAY

I closed the front door behind me. The sky was overcast, the clouds heavy with rain. I had pulled on a blue hoodie to keep me from getting too cold, but the wind sent shivers down my spine with each step.

I checked my phone again. No response yet from Angel. I sighed and looked around. Two girls were in front of me, but they kept looking over their shoulders and whispering. I rolled my eyes, but something in my stomach churned, telling me I was in for something bad. It was probably just the ominous weather, but I had a bad feeling anyway.

I pushed open the door to the library and walked to our table.

"Hey," I said, sitting down.

It was deathly quiet in the room. Perry looked at Thomas, and Natalie was texting on her phone, just barely paying attention. Brit was busy on her phone as well, and Angel was nervously biting her nails.

"Um, are you guys okay?" I asked.

Perry took a side glance at Thomas, then at Brit.

"We're fine," Thomas said flatly, getting out of the chair. "Perfectly fine."

Thomas walked towards the door, leaving the room. The others followed in quick succession.

"Wait!" I cried out, standing up.

They ignored me.

When the door slammed, I was standing alone and confused at our library table. I pulled out my phone instantly, hovering over Angel's contact.

Me:

Angel! What was that about? Did I do something wrong?

No response.

Me:

Angel? Whatever it is I did, I'm so sorry! Can you text me, please?

Nothing. Only a read message.

Angel left me on read. She *never* left me on read.

My heart started to beat faster. What was going on?

The first bell shook me out of my frozen state, and I walked alone to homeroom. I could barely hear the noise of people around me and lockers slamming. I sat down in my seat, and I heard snickering and lots of whispering, especially from the popular girls.

Charlene was talking in a hushed voice back and forth to Nina. Perry grinned at her phone from across the room, and Brit giggled as she whispered something into her ear. It must have been funny because Perry burst into laughter.

Natalie was angrily flipping the pages of her book, and Thomas sat silently next to her. I tried to look at him, but he turned away, refusing to make eye contact.

The homeroom bell rang, and Natalie stormed up to my desk. Her face was red and blotchy.

"Alex," she barked. "What the *hell* has gotten into you?"

She gritted her teeth, and there was more laughing behind her.

I thought I heard Nina drawl, "Oh girrrrl."

I looked around for help.

"What did I do?" I asked her, confused.

"Oh, you know what you did," she snapped before turning on her heels and stomping out.

Now the laughing was louder. I tried to run after her, but she was swallowed up by the crowd before I could get to her. What the hell was going on?

·　　·　　·

I walked to second period, nervously sitting at my desk between Perry and Brit.

"What do you think you're doing?" Brit said angrily, storming up to my desk.

"I-I don't understand," I stuttered.

My heart started pounding in my chest. I felt like I was drowning.

"You were always such a suck-up and always in the way," Perry said. *"Oh, Thomas, tell me about swim. Oh, Thomas, do you have some wood blocks I can have? Oh, Thomas, can I come to your island and look in your Nook shop?"* Perry scoffed. "You always were monopolizing him so he wouldn't talk to me." Perry crossed her arms over her chest.

I gasped and started to talk. "What are you—?"

"Shut up," Brit said. "You were clearly just leading him on. And now it's out in the open what a B you are."

Brit strode away, leaving me behind.

What did that even mean? My mind tried to catch up but couldn't. I pinched myself, leading to a wince. Unluckily, it was definitely real.

I quickly pulled out my phone, beginning to text Angel. My heart beat faster as I tried to think of something to say.

"Alex, put your phone away," Mrs. Valerie said, looking at me.

I put it away and was met with some giggles in the room. I tried to look at Angel, but she avoided my gaze the entire class period. Angel would know what to do. Why was she ignoring me? We had been friends forever.

I tried to stop myself from hyperventilating or, worse, crying. The stress and panic consumed me throughout the period, and it was a feat to even pay attention with my stomach knotted up as it was. After the torture, I ran up to Angel as she was about to leave.

"Angel!" I yelled, racing up to her.

I tried to grab her by the arm, but she just turned away, walking fast. She was walking the opposite way from math class, but I had to know what was going on.

I weaved my way through the crowd, trying to find Angel. I could feel my heartbeat in my throat, and tears started to well up. She was nowhere to be found.

Turning around, I pulled out my phone to text her. I had two minutes until the bell rang, silently cursing at myself as I shoved my phone away. I raced to math; there was no way I could be late.

The ear-piercing sound of the bell met me as I audibly cursed. It was right there. Sighing wearily, I put my hand on the door handle to Mr. Koffman's room.

Mr. Koffman didn't comment as I entered. I took a deep breath in and held it before I exhaled, trying to calm myself. Those numbers could protect me.

"Alex, can you show me how—" Raaj started before he looked at my face. "Hey … are you okay?"

"I … um, just something with my friends."

I didn't want to bring this into math class. Raaj would think I was a stupid seventh grader. I exhaled and sat next to him.

"Here, let me show you." I picked up the pencil and just focused on the numbers, trying to let everything else fall away.

. . .

"See you tomorrow," Jay called out as we filed out of the math room.

The cold air of the hallway hit me. I could hear rain outside, pelting the windows with their watery surface. I ran across the grass to the cafeteria, shaking the rain off of me. I attempted not to slip in the puddles forming at the entrance, but it was a struggle.

That's when I started to hear the whispered comments. People would glance at me and then back down at their phones or lean over toward their friends. I walked over to my usual spot. Perry was sitting next to Thomas, with her hand on his arm.

Oh. Now it started to click.

As I put my stuff down on the table, Perry said, "Come on, everyone."

They all stood up, grabbing their lunches and backpacks as they walked away.

I stood there for a moment, trying to catch my breath. I sat down at the large, expansive table. It felt so empty without anyone filling it, and I wasn't close to any of my teachers, so I couldn't hide in any of their rooms. Everyone had already seen my humiliation. Lunch only had seventh graders. If it had been a combined lunch, I would have looked for Raaj or Jay, or anyone from my math class. But they all went to their fourth period and had lunch later.

Ignoring the pain, I pulled out my math homework. It calmed me down a little but didn't make me any happier. I stood up to throw my lunch away, unable to swallow anything. As I got up, Angel bumped into me.

"Oh, I'm so—" she started, the remains of her tomato soup spilling over my shorts.

She cut herself off when she looked up, her eyes meeting mine. Her face looked torn, but she didn't finish her sentence as she strode away, leaving me behind.

My phone began to buzz inside my backpack with *Instagram* notifications. I looked around, horrified to see people taking photos. Just great.

"Angel. Please listen. I don't know what Perry told you—" I begged.

But she had already sprinted off.

Feeling defeated, I walked to the bathroom and quickly changed. Things got spilled often thanks to my clumsiness, so I had packed an extra pair of clothes in case anything were to go south. I splashed some cold water onto my face and the back of my neck, hoping it would calm me down. But much to my dismay, it did hardly anything, and as I looked at the floor, I noticed there were some red spots on my shoes. I grabbed a brown paper towel and wet it, dabbing at the soon-to-be forever stains that would remind me of this crappy day.

I pushed open the bathroom door and began to walk to science class. Just three more periods, and I could fix this over the weekend. I could ask Gwen to drive me to Angel's house. She would have to talk to me then, right? Wouldn't she? My heart started to race. I could barely catch my breath. What was it that Angel had told me about her therapy for anxiety? That's right. In for four, hold for four. I exhaled for four but couldn't hold for another. My breath was too short, which didn't help with the stress much.

I walked into science with my head down, staring at my shoes. They looked like I had cried blood tears on them. People were laughing and talking loudly. Obviously, about me. The teacher turned around from the board, and she tried to stop us.

"Quiet class! Quiet!" Mrs. Harlem snapped.

"Can you believe it?" Charlene said loud enough for me to hear, checking if I was looking, "She told Thomas she *hated* him."

My eyes widened, and it took a minute for that information to register. Then, I jolted from my seat.

"I didn't do that!" I yelled at Charlene, desperately trying to defend myself.

From the other side of the room, I heard, "Yes, you did."

Thomas's eyes flashed with pain.

"But I don't hate you!" I said. "I like you."

Others began giggling. I heard Charlene almost howl with laughter. My face went red.

"I don't mean I … *like* you."

Thomas turned to me, smiling with pain on his face. "Wow. I guess it is really true." He stopped, exhaling as he turned back to face the front of the classroom.

"Alex, sit down," Mrs. Harlem said. "Class, we are going to continue with the rock cycle …"

Charlene lifted up her phone, playing a recording. "Hey, Alex, listen to this!"

She began playing a recording of someone saying they hated Thomas. Saying they weren't friends at all. And the worst part was that it sounded like … me.

My mouth went dry, and I stopped hearing the din around me. I had to fix this. How do I fix this? My breathing sped up. I had to get away, and I stood up and ran for the door. This could not be happening. The tears welled up as I darted across the halls. I wanted to be in Math class again or be at home with Gwen, who always understood me. She would make me feel better. But Gwen wasn't here. I was on my own.

I started feeling dizzy. That wasn't me, but it sounded like my voice.

People in the classroom began to laugh. I stumbled back to the nearest classroom and flung open the door. It was Ms. Young's class, whom I had last year for World History.

I weakly said in the open door, "I'm gonna faint."

Everything became fuzzy around the edges, and I think I saw Ms. Young move towards me. I slid down the wall, my butt landing on the ground. I didn't want to hit my head if I fainted.

And then the world went black.

.   .   .

I woke up in the nurse's office, alone. I reached for the orange juice that was sitting next to the stiff medical bed I was lying on. The sharp tang of the juice cleared my senses, and I did what every seventh grader does when alone. Check *Instagram*. My DMs were flooded with mean comments from Charlene and *The Pops,* as well as hateful comments from my *friends* and complete trash from people I didn't even know. I could feel the bile rising in my throat as I read.

Would the rest of middle school be like this from now on? Would I spend all my days alone and hated? I imagined myself sitting alone on a bench before classes started. Maybe I could ask Mr. Koffman if I could eat lunch in his room, but it wouldn't help that much in the grand scheme of things. My heart beat faster and faster. My head was pounding.

I put my phone away in my pocket and brushed something.

I remembered.

"You'll need it," he said.

"But when?" I asked.

"You'll know."

I had one chance.

I pulled out the jelly bean and ate it.

CHAPTER FOUR AND A HALF – NEW FRIDAY

Each day has its own beginning.

They all start the same way—by waking up.

Everything that happened in the past few days was straight in front of me as my breathing evened. My friends telling me I talked too much and too loudly. Charlene bullying the band girl. Perry always making a snide remark when Thomas was around. Perry talking with Charlene in class. The truth or dare in PE.

I could see it all as a straight line, and I saw my next move. Just like a math equation, there was a clear answer.

And just like that, I woke up.

The nurse came back in, and I told her I wasn't feeling well, asking to stay the rest of the period. She agreed, and after she left, I pulled out my phone again. I knew that, somehow, I needed to get Charlene's attention. She was still stuck in science class while I was halfway across the campus on a rock-hard mattress.

I opened *Instagram*, sifting through Charlene's profile to get some intel. I clicked on her profile picture, only to find a picture of my empty seat in science class with a description:

Caption:
Poor Alex, I bet she called her parents to get picked up from school.

It was infuriating, sure, but I had to keep a level head for this plan to work.

The first thing I did was edit my Close Friends list. I removed Angel, Natalie, and Thomas. I started to feel sad, but I shoved that feeling down. I started adding *The Pops* and a few others who had sent those nasty DMs to me. I snapped a photo, clicked a few filters on *Lightroom*, and wrote:

Caption:
I fake-fainted while you guys did the science test. ;)

I knew that by this point, most people were on their phones, including Charlene's clique. So without hesitation, I posted the story to my new and improved Close Friends list.

I sent a DM to Charlene shortly after.

Me:
That was some quick editing. You got me. If you're done playing with sub-par Brit and Perry, we should talk. You should be able to find a way to get to the nurse's station if you're as smart as I think you are.

What was even going on? How could I talk to Charlene like that? My head was buzzing with questions, shocked at my own words.

Within fifteen minutes, Charlene sauntered into the nurse's station, holding an ice pack to her elbow. There was no way she could resist a challenge like that. I quickly sat on the edge of the mattress, a smirk playing on my lips. Charlene placed the ice pack on the sink and turned toward me with an intrigued yet quizzical expression on her face.

"Smart move, fainting to avoid the science test. But I know you didn't bring me here to gloat. So, why am I on your *Close Friends* list?" she asked.

"I've known my so-called friends since kindergarten. If they don't trust me by this point, they don't deserve to be in my life anymore. People like that aren't worth my time." I flicked an invisible piece of lint off my shirt, trying to look uninterested.

Charlene's eyebrows raised. "Then why did you message me?"

"If you can't beat 'em," I said, standing up and moving closer to her. She took a step back in response. "Then join 'em."

She breathed a *hmph* in acknowledgment. Charlene seemed impressed, or at the very least, trying to calculate her next move. For years, I had seen her as a force to be reckoned with. But here we were, both sizing each other up.

"You're … different. Where's all this confidence coming from?" Charlene crossed her arms tightly, squinting as if she could see right through my sugary-sweet facade.

Before I could answer, the harsh sound of clicking heels crept into the background. The nurse was coming back. I exchanged a knowing look with Charlene.

"Call off your social media dogs, and I'll tell you."

Her eyes sharpened but then relaxed. "Sure … I'll DM you my number. Don't do anything stupid with it."

And with that, Charlene spun around on her Vans and strode quickly out of the nurse's station.

"I wouldn't dare," I said to Charlene's back.

My internal dialogue was fighting itself; one part was telling me to run away from the girl in front of me. After all, she had caused my predicament. But another part was silky smooth, folding its hands together in satisfaction because it had worked.

I wasn't clueless anymore.

I wasn't awkward anymore.

I was a New Alex.

.   .   .

School had ended hours ago, but the lingering feeling of emptiness didn't. The house was quiet, mocking me. Gwen had meetings on Friday and wouldn't be home until later. Even a magical jelly bean couldn't hide my remorse. My friends were gone. My reputation was gone. Anything that had kept me stable was gone. My friends were ignoring my texts. I even logged onto *Animal Crossing* only to immediately log off because they had unfriended me in the game already. We had been tight-knit since elementary, a bunch of nerdy kids with an unbreakable bond. And all it took was a false rumor for our friendship to crack in two.

After another hour, I closed my laptop and rolled away from the desk. Even watching clips of *Tyrants*, my primary coping mechanism, wasn't working. I had already gone for a walk, worked on fanart, did several math equations, and eaten the rest of the *Dove* chocolates. If none of that was making a difference, using the Internet was bound to be futile as well.

I stood up from my chair and trudged into the kitchen to make a cup of tea. I realized Gwen must have come home a while ago. She was sitting on the nearby couch curled up in a fluffy blanket, probably scrolling through a group chat. Usually, I would've done the same. Except nobody was texting me today. I sniffed, trying to ignore the preemptive stinging of tears that hadn't yet been released.

"Alex? Are you okay?"

"I-I'm fine," I said roughly. "Just tired, that's all."

Gwen tried to make eye contact with me from the couch, her eyebrows furrowed in a look of concern. I looked away quickly. All of the mugs in the cabinet were decorated with logos and colorful designs. I picked up one that read *No mourners, No funerals*, a birthday gift from Angel. For half a second, I considered smashing it against a wall, but I knew I'd regret it later. I didn't have the heart to deface Jesper like that.

"Okay … are you getting enough sleep? It's only middle school; you don't have to start ruining your sleep schedule just yet."

I racked my brain for lies as the hot water poured from the coffee machine. Well, it *could* make coffee. But most members of our family found the hot water function much more useful.

"I was catching up on *Tyrants'* streams that I had missed last week. Sorry."

The teabag slid into the swirling liquid, staining the water with orange. I tipped the honey bottle upside down, letting the sweet gold liquid drip for at least a few seconds.

"You know the videos are on the Internet forever, right? They'll still be there when you wake up."

"Well, not everything's permanent!" I said a little too harshly.

The spoon angrily clinked against the mug as I stirred.

"Alex, I don't think this conversation is really about *Tyrants*," Gwen said, starting to stand up.

My voice quivered. "Yes, it is. I'm fine."

Gwen walked up to me and held her arms out. "We don't have to talk about it. Just promise you'll ask for help if you need it, okay? I can ask Mom and Dad about a professional if—"

"I said I'm *fine*." I grabbed my mug, almost burning my fingers, and strode past my sister.

Her face flashed with pain.

After getting back to my room and locking the door, I crawled into my bed. I put in my earbuds, finding the sad playlist I had made the other day. I didn't think I'd be using it so soon.

I pulled my knees up to rest under my chin and sipped the tea slowly. Everything was so, *so* messed up. My friends had abandoned me at the first sign of conflict, Perry and Brit had my friends in their pockets, and *The Pops* were the ones pulling the strings. It was a long, convoluted chain of betrayal. And in the low light, the soft tunes of Olivia Rodrigo surrounded me, opened the dam behind my eyes, and let the tears fall.

CHAPTER FIVE – SATURDAY

"Is there any gum in the car? My breath smells like turkey bacon."

"I have some mints," Mom said, handing a small box of Tic Tacs to Gwen.

"Thanks," Gwen replied as she popped a few into her mouth.

I smiled from the backseat. It was always nice when we were able to spend time together as a family. My parents weren't supposed to work during the weekend, but more often than not, they got called in for an emergency.

Mom opened the glovebox and pulled out a black scrunchie, and promptly tied it around her dark red curls.

"Alright, should we go in?" Dad asked.

"It's still pretty early, but we can go," Mom said, unlocking her car door.

We all got out of the car and walked towards the synagogue. There were a few other families coming, but most people were already inside. I held open the glass door and stepped into the warmly lit lobby area. It was mainly empty, and the echo of the rabbi's voice from the main room was loud and clear.

Dad stopped outside to put on his tallit while mom pinned the lace kippot to the top of her head. We entered the sanctuary and found a place to sit.

I pulled my siddur out of my tote bag, and mom nudged me as the rabbi was speaking.

"Are you reading along?" she whispered to me.

"Yes, I'm trying to," I snapped.

Mom let out a sigh, turning back to the service.

After a lot of sitting and standing and praying, Gwen shot me a look.

"What's up with you? You don't seem like yourself," she whispered.

"It's nothing," I hissed coldly.

"That's kinda suspicious ..." She stated as she pursed her lips and narrowed her eyes at me.

Mom quickly shushed us before we could interrupt the service more, but it bothered me that Gwen might know.

I was quiet the rest of the service and asked if we could leave early because I was starting to get a headache. I dashed into my room before Gwen could ask any more questions.

I opened *Instagram* to see if I had any notifications. There weren't many, and I scrolled through the ones remaining. All the comments making fun of me had stopped around 3:00 yesterday. Charlene definitely did her work then.

But I needed an answer. I took the jelly bean, and I had no idea what it did. What was next?

Maybe I could build up the strength to try out for being an alternate.

I quickly got my purse and my keys, slipping on my shoes as I raced to the door.

"Hey, Mom, I'm going to go for a walk!" I called as I opened the door.

"Alright," she replied, looking up from her report.

I walked out, closing the door behind me as I sighed heavily.

I needed answers.

Racing down the path to school, I stopped at the candy shop. Luckily the lights were on, but it seemed empty. I walked towards it, throwing open the door of the shop as I walked in, almost tripping on the entrance.

The same person who gave me the jelly bean was standing behind the register. He turned around, his eyes running down my body to my shoes and then slowly up. He put the cloth he was using for cleaning down on the countertop.

"I suppose you ate the jelly bean, Alex," he said calmly.

"Yeah," I said. "So, what the heck did that do?"

He smiled. "It does two things. It alters people's perception of you, and the effects get more potent as time goes on."

I was quiet for a few seconds.

"What do you mean, *more potent*?"

He chuckled. "It means you'll get less awkward the longer you have it. The first few days might be a little rough at first. Later on, things will get much easier."

"Oh," I said. "So that explains why Charlene suddenly acted differently around me. I didn't know why she gave me her number. And in the nurse's office, I was really confident and knew what to do. But right now, I have no idea. And—"

He cut me off. "That rambling will also go away."

I snapped my mouth shut. "Umm. You never told me your name."

I looked for a name tag not finding one.

"No, I didn't. Have a great day, Alex. I'll see you next week."

He turned and left the countertop, and went into the backroom. I guessed our conversation was over.

I walked out of the shop, closing the door. It was certainly confusing, but it cleared some things up. I hoped my emotions evened out before I had to speak with the *Queen of Pops*.

.   .   .

When it was finally 4:00, I picked up my phone and punched in Charlene's number.

"Hey," I said coolly when she answered on the third ring.

"Oh, hi," Charlene responded. "What's up with the new change?"

"I just tried something new," I replied casually. "I realized I wasn't really living up to my potential, y'know?"

"Mm-hmm," Charlene said, but she sounded doubtful.

"So, what are you wearing today?" I asked.

I felt like fashion would be a good topic to get the ball rolling.

She paused but then continued. "Well, right now, I'm wearing black pants, a white shirt tucked in but not puffed out, and a jean jacket with full-length sleeves pulled up to three-quarters."

Yikes. I may have had a new way of thinking, but I did not even understand what gibberish she was talking about. I guess the jelly bean didn't come with a popular translator.

"What are *you* wearing?" she asked.

I wished I never brought up fashion.

"Wait one sec," I said.

I started using my new skills to think of a stylish outfit from Gwen's closet.

"Finding a mirror?" she said.

"Yeah. I'm wearing a white half-cut shirt with ripped jeans. Light colored with no specific wash."

Shoot. Now I was speaking gibberish.

"Where'd you buy it?" I could hear her sneer on the other end of the line.

"Bluewave Boutique" I said.

Thank goodness I remembered where Gwen shops.

"Oh …" she said.

She seemed to be getting interested.

"Did you know that shop is owned by Nina's mom?" she shared.

I sat down on my bed, making myself comfortable.

"No. I didn't know that," I admitted with curiosity.

"Nina's mom was like a supermodel when she was young," she added.

"What! No way!" I said, amazed.

"Yep. Anyways, do you wanna stop for some new clothes tomorrow? We're also gonna go to the pool," she said.

"Sounds cool to me," I replied.

"Well, okay then. And just a question. How did you make those filters on *Instagram*? I never saw anything like it."

"Oh, that? That was just a trick I learned. You edit it in *Photoshop Lightroom* with a preset, and then you repost it in *Insta*."

"Huh," she said.

She switched the subject rather than waiting for clarification.

"Did you actually like Thomas?"

My stomach twisted into knots. I took a steady breath before I answered.

"A little, but you kinda ruined that for me. No worries," I said, keeping my voice even and light.

How the heck did I sound like this?

"Oh, well, you can do better than him."

That was uncalled for. And rude.

"Yeah?" I asked, pretending to be interested.

"Red's cousin is pretty cute …"

"Who's that?"

"Adrian. He's on the lacrosse team and actually kinda smart. Now that I think about it, he might be perfect for you."

This sounded promising.

"What's his *Insta*?"

"Sending it to you right now."

I pulled it up. Open smile. Short-cropped hair with warm brown skin. Holding a lacrosse stick with a bit of sweat on his face, as if he just finished a game. Which he probably did at the time the picture was taken.

"I could work with this. How do you want to set this up?"

What were these words coming out of my mouth?

"I'll DM him about you and see if he can meet us tomorrow. I'll make sure those photos from yesterday are gone before I share your *Insta*. But I'll send him a cool photo of you from the nurse's office."

"Thanks," I said. "How come I've never seen him around at school?"

"He's at Oakleaf Middle. He's in the STEM program there. Like I said, he's smart."

Part of my stomach flipped about the idea of meeting a cute guy who was actually smart. And it was exciting to have someone set me up with a guy.

"Sounds cool. So, talk to me about what I should wear to impress him."

.   .   .

I hung up at 4:30 and asked my mom to drive me over to Raaj's since she was home.

After a few minutes of driving, I walked up to Raaj's house.

"Oh hey, Alex!" Raaj said, opening the door.

"Hey. How are you?" I asked.

"Good," he replied.

"Hey!" I heard Jay yell from across the house.

"Oh hey," I said, following Raaj to the couch, where snacks had been set out.

Raaj sat down, handing me a notepad.

"Should we start?"

"Yep," I responded. "So, how's the math team going?"

"Our competition's soon, so I'm slightly nervous about it," Jay said.

"Yeah," Raaj replied. "We practiced some new equations recently, and I'm not super excited to see those at the competition."

It would be so fun to go to a competition, to get out there and solve equations, even if I wasn't actually part of the team.

"Oh, I bet," I said. "I hate learning things last minute."

"I know, right?" Jay replied. "Like, couldn't we just have learned that earlier or something? It's such a pain!"

"And then you have to go through the trouble to make sure you know it. That's a mess. So do you think the rest of your team is good?"

"I think they're pretty decent, but this one boy on our team is such a know-it-all," Raaj groaned. "He keeps trying to boss us around and tell us the equations and stuff."

"Oh, you mean Adam? He's not that bad," Jay commented. "But I do understand the know-it-all thing; they are annoying occasionally."

"I hate know-it-alls. But they don't really bother me as much," I said.

"Oh hey, do you want to see a movie with us tomorrow? A new movie came out, and we have an extra ticket," Raaj said.

"Yes! Ooh …" My mind remembered the conversation with Charlene less than an hour ago. "I think I might be busy," I said. "I'm so sorry."

"It's fine," Jay replied. "Anyways, we should probably start."

I nodded as Jay pulled out a pack of question cards with equations messily written in faded pencil. We began the questions, going past the first few quickly, but my mind was buzzing, nervous about the next day and my new popularity.

"Alright, so the question is … 1,556 cubed," Jay said.

"Hmmm …" Raaj thought. "Not sure. What about you, Alex?"

I was so consumed in my own thoughts I could barely hear him.

"Oh, what?" I asked.

"What's the answer?"

I froze. I didn't hear it. "Can you repeat it? I'm kind of tired today."

"Oh sure," Jay replied. "It's 1,556 cubed."

"It's … 3,797,587,216 … I think," I replied.

"Incorrect … are you okay? You seem kind of weird today. You've been getting the past few wrong …"

I rushed to my defense. "What! I'm fine! I promise."

I sighed, trying to focus. I was able to get the right answers, but it seemed … harder. The lack of sleep had to be catching up with me. I doubted the jelly bean caused it, but I still wasn't entirely sure how it worked.

When I was home, I regretted not listening. I had been so excited, and I just blew it. There was no way I could ask to be an alternate now. I sighed. Something was off. That study session was the only thing that emotionally got me through the week, and it wasn't fulfilling. At all.

I logged onto *Minecraft* to begin playing. I went onto Angel's server, quickly loading in. To be honest, I was surprised I wasn't banned. I looked around the world where I last left off. I moved my mouse to look around the underground cavern carved out with TNT. I had textured the walls and floors, so it was more interesting to look at, and small buildings peeked out from holes in the cave. I quickly switched tabs, switching to Spotify as I turned on a song, *Right Now* by *Confetti.* I bobbed my head to the music as I began collecting resources and fixing up the place.

I only wanted to stay online for so long just in case Angel logged on and banned me. That wouldn't be good. I walked through the base, running across an explosion, a sign deliberately left in the middle.

I sighed. Of course, my friends griefed my base.

I removed the sign that read a crude message signed by Perry and Brit. I just left the hole where my base used to be. If I fixed it, they would just blow it up again. My stomach churned. I felt sad about losing my friends. There was just a hole in my stomach where they used to be.

Just another sign a piece of me was missing.

CHAPTER SIX – SUNDAY

What did that jelly bean even do?

Sure, it helped with the whole 'being awkward' situation, but everything was just so … complicated. Would things get worse or better or something entirely different? It was such a stupid decision to make, and the dread of it twisted my stomach into knots.

I was glad Gwen slept in on Sundays because I did not want her to find out. The jelly bean was already consuming my mind, and it would be worse to add Gwen on top of that pile of guilt. She was already suspicious of me, and I didn't want it to escalate.

I put on my striped, blue one-piece swimming suit and heard the car horn beep outside. Trying to forget about my dilemma, I started to pack my things in a rush. I locked the door behind me and jogged over to the sleek SUV parked on the street. A woman rolled down the window as I approached.

"Oh, hello, Alex. Nice to meet you," Ava's mom said.

"Oh, hi. Nice to meet you too," I replied, getting into the backseat with Charlene.

"It's so nice that Ava's making new friends," She chirped.

"Mhm …" Ava mumbled a little uncomfortably.

I was uncomfortable, too. Sure, I knew Ava from the project, and she was relatively nice, but I hadn't really gotten to know any of *The Pops* that well. Two days ago, they had set me up, and I wasn't even sure what I was doing here. The silence was suffocating, and after a few minutes, Ava plugged in her phone to the AUX cord, pulling up some music.

"Do you have any suggestions?" Ava asked.

"No. I'm fine with anything," I replied.

Charlene didn't seem to have a preference either.

Ava flipped through her playlist, selecting a song. The melody began playing, and the song title showed on the car screen in the front. *Body and Mind* by *girl in red*. With the silence cut, the tension faded. I could see Ava silently humming the lyrics and her mom bobbing her head to the song as well.

Ava's mom parked in a reserved spot.

"Here's the keycard. Don't lose it," she warned. "I have some errands to run, but just text when you need a pickup."

I grabbed my swimming bag and followed them into the pool. I realized this was the *400 Club*, where Thomas swam. I started to get nervous and hoped that he wasn't here. Or maybe I was hoping he would be here and we could talk.

The pool was Olympic size, and it made sense the swim team rented time. The sun-kissed water shone a gorgeous aquamarine blue and stretched on for what seemed like miles. Talking filled the air, and a soft breeze flew through my hair. Some bouncy music echoed in the wind.

"Hey over here!" Nina yelled over to us.

They were sitting on an almost completely empty part of the pool where they had laid out towels on the concrete and put a few on the lounge chairs. We walked over and sat down.

"Thanks for saving those seats for us," I commented.

"Not a problem," Charlene said, slathering on a huge amount of sunscreen.

"That's a lot of sunscreen," I said.

"I know. My skin just burns so much in the sunlight."

I was about to say that she looked fine, but Nina caught sight of someone in the distance and pursed her lips, letting out a scoff.

"Her again?" Ava asked, but Nina just kept pouting.

I looked at the person they were staring at. It was a girl, tall and slender, black curly hair flowing down her brown skin. She wore a violet swimsuit and silver sandals that glimmered in the sunlight.

"Who's that?" I asked.

"Ryder Atrion," Nina snarled. "She's suddenly my rival competition in Birchwood. She's just so … ugh."

I saw a small crowd flocking around Ryder as she walked by confidently, standing tall and straight.

She tripped on a puddle of water and was flocked with people crowding to help her up.

And then I saw a tin roll out from behind the crowd. Ryder frantically grabbed it, shoving it back into her bag.

My eyes widened knowingly as I remembered her from the candy store.

"Hey, Ryder! How's that working for ya?" the cashier had asked her.

"It's going great! The stuttering's gone. It really works!" She had replied.

Nina looked over somewhere else. "Hey, Red! Come over here!"

The person caught sight of us and walked over. There was another person standing next to him.

Charlene nudged me. "There he is," she said, waving at the other person next to Red.

Adrian looked way cuter in real life than I thought. They spotted us and walked over.

Nina jumped up from the seat and into Red's arms. I got up from my seat and walked towards Adrian, making sure we were out of earshot from the others just in case I said something awkward.

"Hey," I said evenly, looking up at him.

"Hey," he said back.

He took off his sunglasses, revealing his hazel eyes.

"I … umm … got this new bathing suit. What do ya think?"

His smile turned downward. "Um … it looks good on you."

"Yeah?" I asked, waiting for him to compliment me.

What was coming out of my mouth? This new personality was ruining this. I had barely even gotten to know the guy, and I was bombing it.

Adrian rubbed the back of his neck, looking down at his sandals. "Um … I'm on the math team at my school. Charlene told me you like math …"

"OMG, you are?" I blurted out. "I was probably gonna sign up soon. I can't believe you're doing it! That's so cool! Which math are you doing in practice? I kinda wanna know what questions they ask in competitions."

His smile returned along with a dimple. "We're doing algebra. Not pre-algebra, but normal algebra. It's one of our main focus points, but we do some geometry also."

"That's awesome!"

"Yeah," he said. "It's pretty fun."

There was an awkward pause for a few seconds.

I cleared my throat. "Hey, I heard you played lacrosse; how is it?"

"It's fun, but you really get beat up. And then your coach is yelling the whole time to keep moving while you're fainting from the heat."

"It's Florida. What do you expect?"

We both burst out laughing.

"Hey, is that a *Perry the Platypus* sticker on your bag?" I asked him.

He turned a little red. "Yeah. It's a little embarrassing, but I watched *Phineas and Ferb* when I was a kid, and sometimes, I still do 'cause it's still a little funny."

I smiled, taking a breath, singing the familiar theme. "There's a hundred and four days—"

"Of summer vacation," Adrian responded.

I laughed. "Y'know, there have been times I was able to get through the entire song with all of my friends."

"Now that's a feat," he said. "Most of my friends didn't watch the show, so they don't know about it."

"Look, if your friend is able to sing the entire *Phineas and Ferb* theme in sync with you—they're a winner."

I remembered singing the song with Natalie and Angel on the fifth-grade *Legoland* field trip. I shook my head to push away the memory.

"Exactly. My standards precisely," he said brightly.

"Did you know that *Phineas and Ferb* is being renewed for two seasons?"

Adrian's eyes widened. "Wait. What?"

"Yeah! Dan Povenmire posted a video on *Instagram* announcing it," I explained.

"That's so cool! I'm excited to see what they do with it."

I glanced at his bag again.

"Oh my god, is that a *Bueno Nach—*"

Adrian broke in, "Okay. Don't judge." He walked over to where everyone was sitting and put his bag down. "Let's swim, and we can discuss how Wade never leaving his house made him the most prepared person for COVID."

. . .

I heard Charlene yell from behind me.

"Hey, Alex! We have to go clothes shopping! Wrap it up, okay?"

"Sure!" I yelled back.

I turned back to Adrian.

"So, I'll see you later then?" I asked.

"Sure," he said, grinning. "Hey, DM me later, okay?"

"Oh, yeah. Definitely, I'll see you," I said, running towards Charlene.

The girls and I used the pool's tiny showers, dried off, and then changed in one of the other rooms. Our hair was wet, but Mallory found hair dryers in one of the cabinets below. We stood there for twenty minutes drying our hair because Charlene said wet hair makes you look terrible. I didn't think I had ever dried my hair for longer than three minutes before then.

Ava's phone dinged just about when Charlene put down the hairdryer.

"My mom's outside," Ava announced.

All of *The Pops* trailed out to the SUV. Mallory pulled the backseat forward, so she could crawl into the third row. There was just enough room for all of us.

"Keycard?" Ava's mom asked, looking at Ava.

Ava pulled it from her bag and placed it in the glove box.

"Thanks for picking us up."

"Yeah, thanks, Mrs. Blackman," Nina called from the back row.

"Yes. Thanks so much," I added.

Ava's mom drove us to a shop that was nestled in a small part of town, next to a quaint-looking wedding shop and a stationary store.

The store looked homey when I stepped inside. Clothes were displayed on wooden racks, and a few changing rooms were a few paces away. There was a backroom where sewing machine sounds could be heard. Near the side of the store was a table with a water infuser dispenser and a tea machine. A few porcelain cups were laid out, and a sign that read in neat cursive, *Please do not let liquid near the garments. Enjoy the refreshments!*

"Whoa, this place is pretty high-end," I commented, glancing at the refreshment table with velvet chairs.

The place seemed so quiet inside. Relaxing music was playing from somewhere in the store, but the whole place seemed very calming.

"It's really cool, right?" Nina grinned, grabbing a glass of citrus-infused water. She took a sip. "Oooh, nice flavor today."

"So, wait, your mom owns the store? Does she make the clothes in it?" I asked, beginning to wander around.

"Yeah," Nina said. "She started making the designs for the clothes, but she never made them herself. She got her friends and other seamstresses to help, and they started the store thanks to the funds she got from her supermodel days," Nina said, finishing the glass of water.

"It's pretty cool, I guess," Charlene mumbled, beginning to examine the clothes.

"Wait, is this where you get your clothes from, Charlene?" I asked. "You said you knew some people, so were you talking about this?" I asked.

"Partly, yes," Charlene said. "I know some other people that make really good clothes, too, though."

"Oh, alright," I said, beginning to explore.

Ava and Mallory were long gone. I wandered over to an aisle that advertised itself as an *artsy look*. I wasn't too familiar with boutiques or aesthetics as a whole, but the colorful clothes and bright patterns drew my attention. I ran into Mallory in the aisle. She was examining a white embroidered blouse and a matching set of tangerine corduroy pants.

"That's an interesting combination," I commented, stepping over near her.

"Yeah. I don't think I'll wear it mainly because my grandmother says orange doesn't fit with my skin tone. Oh, I'm Choctaw, by the way. Wasn't entirely sure if I mentioned that."

"I think it would look good on you," I commented. "And no, I didn't know that."

Mallory opened her mouth to reply, but she caught sight of my empty hands, and concern flashed across her face.

"You don't have anything … need help finding stuff?" she offered.

I sighed in relief. "Definitely. I'm totally lost. I hope it's not a problem."

"Oh, of course not. Here I saw this really cute outfit in the *vintage style* section. I don't know if it fits your style, but it looks so cute …."

After a bit of looking around, we found a few nice outfits. There were some cool jeans and embroidered blouses, and even a plaid overall dress that looked really cute on me. I wasn't really an overalls kind of person, but we all agreed it was a flattering choice.

After a while of looking around with Mallory, I went to the counter, beginning to do the mental math in my head to make sure I had enough money to pay for what I wanted. Mallory suggested about six or so outfits, and I started to put some back.

Charlene stopped me and said, "They all look cute. Bring them."

"Oh, um, it's fine. I don't need all of—"

Charlene stopped me. "Look. I know, like a few days ago, you didn't really care what you wore, and nobody noticed you. But you have some quality stuff right now, and I will not be caught talking to you if you're wearing the normal stuff you wear."

My cheeks turned red in embarrassment.

"O-Oh, okay. I guess I'll buy them then," I stuttered quickly, relocating the outfits and rushing back to the counter.

What would I tell Mom? I would have to make an excuse that I was using the emergency credit card. I would be so dead. I remembered the pin code, but that wouldn't end well. Clothes were so expensive, and even though Mom was a doctor, I probably would get grounded. Was that worth it? Maybe taking the jelly bean wasn't such a good idea.

"Hello. Can you put all of this on my account?" Nina said, gesturing to the pile of clothes.

The cashier immediately recognized Nina, smiling. "Of course."

The woman began to ring up the clothes.

"Nina," I said cautiously. "That's really sweet, but are you sure?"

She waved me off. "Of course. Just tell people that you got it from my mom's store. Good advertising. Oh. And make sure you wear that dress during our Civics presentation," she winked.

I almost audibly sighed in relief. The cashier finished placing the clothes in hanging bags and handed them to each of us.

We stopped for a few seconds at the refreshments table, grabbing to-go cups of tea.

"I think that was a successful shopping venture," Ava said, grabbing a steaming cup of jasmine tea.

"Agreed," Charlene said.

Nina took a sip from a glass of water. "There are some other stores to visit. Want to stop by, or are we done for today?"

"I think we could go to lunch," Ava said. "I brought some extra cash."

"Oh yes!" Charlene said. "I would kill for a hot dog right now."

"Yup," Mallory sighed. "Shopping makes you so hungry."

We placed our orders online for *Shake Shack*. On our way, we passed an ornate outdoor fountain with a fish spraying water up in the middle. A *Barnes & Noble* sat nearby, which Mallory immediately ran to.

"Oh my gosh, Ava, here's the Alice Oseman comic you were looking for!" Mallory said, rushing to the display.

Ava's face brightened, coming over. "Oh my, really?" Ava turned to Charlene. "I have to buy this. I've been looking for months!" she said excitedly.

"Ooh, I bet they have the third installation of *Umbrella Academy*," Mallory said excitedly.

"I have no idea why you like that fandom so much," Ava smirked.

"Well, sometimes I need a break from eight-hundred-page books!"

"Weird flex, but okay," I grinned, walking over to the display.

Charlene groaned. "We don't have time for this."

"Charlene, we have ten minutes until our order's done," Nina commented, glaring at Charlene.

"It doesn't matter. We have to go," Charlene said, storming off. It was clear Ava and Mallory were bummed, but they followed silently back to the *Shake Shack*.

Ava's phone dinged on the way over, so we grabbed our food before sitting at the green wooden picnic table.

"So …" Charlene said, resting her chin on her hand, leaning forward, "since your lame old friends dumped you, and you probably don't care about them anymore, what are their deepest secrets?" She grinned wickedly.

Mallory and Nina nodded in interest, but Ava stayed deathly silent.

It was tempting to spill, but I wasn't that kind of person.

"No," I said evenly. "Their secrets aren't mine to tell." I popped a fry into my mouth.

Charlene narrowed her eyes but didn't say anything. She rolled her eyes and began to ask Nina how things were going with Red before taking a bite of her burger.

I looked carefully at each of them and tried to make sense of how all of them fit. Did they fall into a friendship because they were at the same snack table, or did Charlene pick them because they would fit well together? Where did I fit in? In another world, I could have seen myself talking with Mallory about math or books with Ava.

I turned to Nina when there was a break in the conversation, "Hey. Thanks again for the clothing assist. That was really awesome of you. I wouldn't have been able to spend so much without getting grounded. And the clothes are beautiful."

Nina paused, looking at me before speaking. "Yeah. Sure. I'm glad you like them." She looked down and paused before saying, "I'll tell my Mom you liked them. She loves it when my friends gush over the designs." She stood up. "I gotta use the bathroom. I'll be right back, y'all."

I looked over at *The Pops,* and the sting of losing my old friends didn't hurt as much. But at the same time, it felt like something was missing. Obviously, I was missing my old friends, but it just felt odd. After all, it'd been a pretty great day.

CHAPTER SEVEN – MONDAY

Today was the race. I saw the morning text from Charlene about what to wear. I picked out a stylish outfit of ripped white jeans, as well as a puffed-out light-yellow shirt made of soft fabric with short sleeves, following the suggestion in the message. I snapped a photo of my outfit and sent it to the group. They sent back thumbs up, and I smiled to myself.

I grabbed the toast Gwen had left out for me.

"Hey, you look really good," Gwen called while she was getting food from the fridge.

"Oh, thanks," I said.

I shoved the toast in my mouth and started to pack my backpack.

"I didn't see you yesterday. Today is *The Week*, right? Are you excited?"

I nodded but didn't make eye contact. "Yeah. It should be good. Different from last year. I gotta run, Gwen. Thanks for the toast!"

Gwen frowned. "Alex, what's going on—"

I dashed out the door before she could finish her sentence. I loved Gwen, but I couldn't talk to her about this. She would tell me to try to work it out with my old friends. But they didn't want me, and I couldn't face that hurt again.

I walked along the concrete, and then I saw four people in the distance I couldn't miss.

"Hey, Pops! Wait up!" I yelled after them.

Charlene turned around and said, "What did you call us?"

"Pops," I said smoothly. "That's what people call you because you're popular. You know, cool."

Charlene's face relaxed, and then she said, "Oooooh. I like that. We are *The Pops*."

We all giggled.

"So … you guys ready for the race today?" I asked.

"Oh yeah," Ava said. "I was born ready."

"Totes. I could definitely lose some weight," Nina agreed.

"Race is my middle name," Charlene bragged.

"Yeah. So am I," Mallory said softly.

She looked down at her feet and kicked a pebble.

Before we walked into the school, Charlene said we needed to take a group photo. We all smiled at the screen, and she snapped a picture. She posted it, and I felt the ding in my pocket.

When we got to the school, the gossip about me was different. No longer was it that I was awkward or liked someone. Now the gossip was that *The Pops* had been hazing me to see if I was cool enough for their group, and pretending to pass out was their final test. The entire narrative had been rewritten.

I was confident.

I was smooth.

And suddenly, I was popular.

.   .   .

After changing into my gym clothes, I located Charlene and Nina on the field. I might have looked cute in my new clothes, but I still looked weak in my uniform. Charlene and Nina looked like they ran cross-country.

"I don't know how you both make gym clothes look good," I said.

Charlene giggled, and Nina struck a pose to show off her thigh muscles. I laughed and lightly shoved her.

I looked over my shoulder, and my smile fell. I saw Natalie and Thomas walking toward the tug-of-war event. Natalie looked confused and leaned over to say something to Thomas, who sent me a mean look. I sighed.

Charlene shoved my shoulder with her own. "Don't think about them. It'll be over soon. Come on, let's get some food."

"Um, I'm good. We shouldn't eat food before the race," Nina said.

"Alright," Charlene said. "But I'm starving. Alex, Ava? Could you maybe grab us some hot dogs?"

"Sure," Ava said. "Nina, are you sure you don't want one?"

"Yes. Positive," Nina said.

"Suit yourself," I said, grabbing money out of my pocket.

Ava grabbed a few dollars from hers as well. We walked to the hot dog food truck, standing in front of it. The smell of meat and grease got caught in the wind, making somewhat of a delectable aroma.

The menu displayed several different versions of hot dogs, each with various toppings. I read the menu carefully, but luckily they were all kosher.

"So, which one are you getting?" I asked, looking at Ava.

"Probably just a plain one," Ava said. "Charlene doesn't really care, and neither does Mallory, so I'm just gonna get some condiment packets and call it a day."

"Sounds good to me," I said. "But I'll probably get sauerkraut on mine or something."

"Nice," Ava said. "I never really tried sauerkraut."

"It's pretty good," I commented as the next people in line walked away with freshly made hot dogs. "Very sour, though. But that's why I like it."

"I like spicy things more," Ava said. "But I don't really want to put hot sauce on a hot dog," she grinned.

I chuckled. "I bet someone has, though."

A glance of a familiar face stopped me.

I looked back at Ava, my jaw clenched.

"What's wrong?" Ava asked, looking at me.

She didn't glance behind her. Probably because she didn't want anyone to seem suspicious.

"It's Brit and Perry," I said, my gut churning. "Maybe you're friends with them, but they still trashed my old friend group a bit."

"Oh them?" Ava said. "I never really liked them. We'll just get our hot dogs and get out of here. I'll make sure they don't mess with you."

I paused. "No. I want to talk to them," I said.

"What?"

I handed Ava the money. "Get the hot dogs, okay? I want to do this."

"Alright," Ava said cautiously. "If you need help, I won't be far."

I took a deep breath, turning around. Perry and Brit were standing behind me, snickering as Brit typed on her phone.

"Hey," I said flatly, looking directly at Perry.

"What is it?" she asked, bored.

As I thought of something to say, I noticed Perry was eating a pretzel.

I snatched it out of her hand, taking a bite where she hadn't eaten it.

"Hey, what was that for?" she demanded.

"Oh," I said casually, taking a bite out of the salty crust. "Taking something I wanted. I thought that's how you did things, no?"

"I didn't do that!" Perry yelled.

"You did. You take things no matter the cost. I learned that pretty early on," I said coldly.

"I—" Perry started, but I cut her off.

"So … let me sum up. I was friends with Thomas, and he paid attention to me. You couldn't get his attention on your own, so you had to sabotage my entire social life. You went to destroy friendships I had had for eight years. All because you couldn't get a boy to look at you. You. Are. Pathetic."

Perry turned red as Brit looked at her while she tried to form a response. I strode away from them, feeling a bit better.

We saw Mallory red-faced and talking with Coach Hill. Nina pointed her chin in that direction, and we walked over.

"What's going on?" I asked Charlene.

"Not sure. Mallory's arguing with the coach," Charlene replied.

"Why do I have to wear these gym shorts?" Mallory asked.

She seemed flustered, and her voice was high-pitched.

"You have to. It's standard criteria," our coach said.

"Well, whatever, we shouldn't even have criteria anyway," Mallory argued.

"Did you just talk back to me?" Coach asked, narrowing their eyes.

"Yeah. Yeah, I did," Mallory challenged, picking at her nail polish.

This was unusual sass, even for a *Pop*. Charlene stopped walking, giving them a safe distance.

"You have to wear them to be part of the event. I don't even know why you're arguing about this," Coach said in an exasperated tone.

"Because the uniforms are ugly, that's why. And they are really too short. What would the PTA say about them?" Mallory asked.

"Oh, I give up!" Our coach said. "Head to the principal's office. Right. Now."

"Seriously?" Mallory seemed oddly happy about the circumstance.

"Now," the coach said firmly. She took the slip and left. I looked at Charlene and Nina, who just shrugged.

"Well, now we know what happened to Mallory," Nina said.

"Yeah, I'll text her later. Let's go find Ava. We will need her for the relay race," Charlene said.

·   ·   ·

When I got home, I was still in my grimy gym clothes. I didn't want to put my nicer clothes on until I was clean. Before taking a shower, I called Mallory to see what was up. Mom and Dad were out, and Gwen still wasn't home.

She picked up on the first ring. "Hello?"

"Hey, Mallory? About today …" I began. "I know I don't know you well, but that seemed … off."

"I can't tell you," Mallory said.

"Hey. It's fine if you can't. But I know something's bothering you."

There was a long pause, and then Mallory said, "You're the first one to call me today."

My eyes widened at that. Charlene said she was going to text her.

"Well, I'm avoiding the shower and standing here with dirt all over me. Maybe the others decided to shower first?"

Mallory's laugh was hollow. "I doubt that."

Another long pause.

I continued cautiously, "Sooo … do you want to talk?"

"I'll slip it. But you have to promise not to tell," she said.

"I promise," I said.

"On your life?'

"Uh … not on my life, but I swear I won't tell."

I looked around for someplace to sit so that I wouldn't get dirty. I gave up and sat down on the kitchen tile floor.

"Alright, fine," she whispered. She took a deep breath and blurted, "I cut."

"Like you cut class?" I asked.

I was pretty confused.

"No," she said, exasperated. "I cut … *myself.* Usually, my upper thighs so people can't see it. But those stupid shorts today …"

I said nothing; my brain was spinning.

"What? But … why?" I muttered.

Mallory sighed and continued, "I cut because … well … it just helps me feel better. My parents are pressing me 'bout good grades and … you may think I'm the smartest girl in the school, but … I'm not." She paused, exhaling like she had never talked about this before. "Charlene probably got it going around, so I'd be special. But I'm not special. It's even worse because my older brother goes to Harvard, and my parents are always asking me why I can't be like him."

Mallory started to speak faster like she couldn't get the words out fast enough. "They keep asking if anyone has better grades than me at our school and why I didn't get more than 100% on a test. They tell me I'm not pretty enough and I should just try harder. I just get overwhelmed and feel like I don't have control over anything." She took a long pause before continuing, "So, I take a small razor and rub it against my skin. Nothing really deep. Just enough so I can feel something other than judgment."

This was serious.

"Mallory … how long has this been happening?"

"A year."

My mind probably blew up. A year! If she was feeling like this for more than two weeks, then she had …

"You have depression," I blurted.

It wasn't a question.

She sighed. "I've never been diagnosed, but probably," she responded.

Never been diagnosed? Her parents would probably be worried and would get her a therapist.

"Did you tell your parents?" I asked.

She scoffed. "No. Of course not. This would just be something else they could judge me for."

"But why does this relate to the gym shorts?" I asked.

"I accidentally made one cut too low. If I wore shorts, everyone would see it."

"Hey, Mallory?"

"Yeah?" she asked.

"I won't tell. But you need to get some type of help. A year is too long. Do you think your brother would listen? Maybe Ms. Philips, the guidance counselor? I can go with you if you want support. We can tell people we are going to her for a school project or something."

"I'll think about it. Thanks for listening. I should go. Bye."

"One more thing!" I said quickly.

"Yeah?" she asked.

"Why'd you tell me?"

She paused. "The other day, when Charlene asked about your friend's secrets, you didn't tell her. If you didn't tell her about your old friends, why would I be any different?"

I was silent for a few seconds.

"Mallory, thanks for trusting me and telling me this."

Where did that maturity come from? Gwen had to be rubbing off on me.

Mallory was quiet for a second, and I could hear some tears.

"No one's ever really listened to me, let alone thanked me. No one has ever called to just ask what was wrong. People just assume things are always fine with me." I heard her blow into a tissue. "I'll think about going to the guidance office this week. Bye."

As soon as I hung up, my mind was swarming with questions. I quickly took my shower, a headache starting. While I was squeezing the water out of my hair, my phone beeped, and I picked it up. Adrian was texting me; I totally forgot we had made plans to meet at a local cafe. Oh crap, my phone call had lasted that long?

I threw on my clean clothes from the morning and dashed into the kitchen. I slid across the tile floor.

"Gwen! Can you drive me?"

Gwen looked up from making a sandwich, the knife still coated in mayonnaise.

"Go where?"

"I have a date! C'mon!" I exclaimed frantically, snatching my set of keys from the countertop and filling up my water bottle.

Gwen abandoned the sandwich and ran out after me. She slipped into the driver's seat while I climbed into the passenger seat. Gwen adjusted the mirrors.

"Oooooh, a date? Who's the lucky person? Is his name Thomas—"

"No, no, it's not Thomas," I snapped.

Gwen looked like I slapped her. She put the car in reverse.

"Well, who is it then? Do I even know them?"

Gwen shifted into drive, exiting the neighborhood with only a few turns.

"His name is Adrian, but he's at a different school. Turn right; we're going to the *Citrus Cafe*."

Gwen made the turn, and streetlights flew by in a blur of dark lines.

"Okay, I definitely don't know this kid. What happened to Thomas?"

"He's … he's, uh, he likes someone else."

"Damn, I'm sorry. At least you've got some other prospects."

"Yeah, I guess. Can you drop me off here?" I said as the car pulled up in front of the establishment.

Gwen put the car into park.

"Remember to get a photo of him. And his number. And use your elbow if things go wrong."

"I'll be fine! Keep your phone on so I can text you when I'm ready to go."

Gwen nodded. I exited the car and walked into the cafe, hearing the *vroom* of Gwen's car as it sped away.

I pushed open the glass doors, which were covered in painted slices of oranges and lemons. The whole cafe was decorated in warm tones. Pink egg chairs sat next to orange wooden tables. Yellow coasters and green rugs were scattered throughout. It smelled like citric acid and looked like a package of those fruit jelly slices I ate by the dozens on Passover.

Adrian was sitting at a circular table for two; a tall drink and pastry bag sat next to him. I stepped into the crowded line and browsed the display case. Cucumber sandwiches and croissants filled the glass; they served some regular cafe food in addition to their more iconic, brand-related meals.

"Welcome to the *Citrus Cafe*; what can I do for you?" the cashier asked. She was wearing a bright green apron over a white shirt and long earrings with clay lime slices dangled over her shoulders. Luckily, she looked less ominous than the candy store person and probably wouldn't be selling any magical anti-awkward lemonade.

"I'll just get the large *Pretty in Pink* with a *Legally Blonde Lemon*

Cookie." One of the reasons I loved this cafe was because every menu item was a movie reference, and Gwen and I had tried everything on the menu, sometimes getting items and eating them while watching the movies they depicted.

I handed the cashier a $20 and gave her my name. Then I sat down at Adrian's table.

"Hey, hot stuff," I said confidently.

"What?" Adrian looked around. "What's burning?"

"I-I was talking about … never mind," I fumbled.

The date hadn't lasted for even a minute, and the stupid jelly bean was interfering!

I switched topics quickly. "So, which drink is that?"

"I got a *Wednesday.* It's been forever since I've seen *Mean Girls,*" Adrian admitted.

The drink in front of him was magenta ombre with sugar across the rim. It definitely looked like something *The Pops* would get. Or, I guess what I would get now that I was one of them.

It still felt weird that I was a *Pop.* I never saw myself like that, but now with the jelly bean, things just felt so different. They used to be my enemies, my rivals, and now I was part of their group.

"Same here! Maybe we could plan a movie night."

"As long as we have these drinks."

"I'm sure we can curate a movie-themed menu—"

"Two items for Alex!" The cashier interrupted.

I smiled at Adrian and walked to pick up my food. After a few careful steps so as to not spill the drink, I sat back down.

"Oh, those look good!"

"Yeah. My sister and I think this is the best meal combo so far. I haven't started using legal jargon in everyday language yet, but it's just a matter of time," I smiled, chuckling a bit.

"Well, I have to disagree. This drink is clearly better," Adrian taunted, taking a sip through the colorful straw.

"Objection!"

"Oh no, the drink has poisoned your vocabulary," Adrian laughed a bit.

We both grinned and broke into full laughter.

"So, how was your school day?" I asked carefully.

Even with new social skills, I had no idea how to flirt. Or at least, how to flirt so it sounded authentic. At least references were safe.

"Tiring. My reading teacher gave us two essays to do in the next week!"

"What? That's ridiculous. Are you still going to that class tomorrow?" I smiled.

Adrian sighed. "I don't know if I'm emotionally ready," he winked.

I leaned back in my chair, impressed. "Wow, okay. You really do know your movie references. I'm gonna have to up my game."

Adrian leaned in, his face more serious. "I don't think so. I think that your game is pretty strong."

I blushed, unsure what to say. His eyes were such a beautiful shade of hazel, with flecks of green scattered through. Is that what flirting was? Was I flirting? I realized that I was decidedly not flirting because now I was sitting there completely quiet after he made that comment which made my heart race.

"You're cute when you blush," he smirked.

I could feel my cheeks becoming even warmer.

"Hang tight; I'm gonna get myself a cookie. Then I'm going to ask a bunch of questions so I can get to know you better."

He sauntered off to the counter, and I watched him walk. I put my hand on my chest and willed my breathing to slow down, and thought three things. First, he thought I was cute. Me! Second, he wanted to get to know me. Me again! And third, I shared kindergarten snacks with the last people who wanted to get to know me.

CHAPTER EIGHT – TUESDAY

The next morning I checked my texts. No events for *The Week* were planned for today. Just a smooth, normal day. But I was still popular and still confused about what Mallory told me the day before, so it wasn't completely normal. I held my phone tightly as I checked *Instagram*. Adrian and I had taken a lot of photos, both of our drinks and each other. Yesterday evening, I posted an image of him, face frozen in a bright smile, with the **caption,** "Cute date and fun drinks! Can't wait for next time." It had only been one night since I uploaded, but the number of likes was triple what I normally got in the pre-*Pops* era. There were quite a few DMs asking me about the date, as well. I'd have to respond to those later.

I pulled on a coral top with my belly button showing. My shoulders were bare, with spaghetti straps crossing over my neck. I also picked some dark gray jean shorts to complete the look. I snapped a pic for Charlene, who quickly responded with a heart.

Flipping through my phone messages and realized I missed a text yesterday from Raaj.

Raaj:
Extra practice after school today? You available?

Shoot, I didn't even see that. I started to text back but decided I would just talk to him in class.

I decided to wear my new cerulean *Vans* with white side details and popped some gum in my mouth, yelling out to Gwen that I was going to skip breakfast and would see her later. I closed the door before she could respond.

My stomach growled at missing the pancakes, but Ava texted she was bringing bagels and we could eat on the way to school. I promised myself that I would catch up with Gwen after I was finished with school. I needed to tell her what was going on with me.

.   .   .

When I got to reading class, Charlene called me over to sit next to her.

"New seating chart," she motioned to the front of the classroom.

"Again?" I said.

But I breathed a sigh of relief. I never wanted to sit near Perry or Brit again. I sat next to Charlene, and she motioned for me to look at my phone.

I knew it was against the rules, but I didn't want to ignore Charlene's texts, and I wanted to see what Mallory said about going to the guidance counselor. I tried to balance paying attention and the text messages. Mallory wouldn't commit to going to the guidance counselor, and I was still worried.

When I got to math, I was still texting.

Charlene:
Hey Alex?

Me:
Yeah? What's up?

Charlene:
You got any plans? Me and Mallory are going to the mall. You in?

I was about to text my response when Raaj stopped me.

"What are you doing?" he whispered, referring to my texting and not doing the warm-up equation.

"It's an emergency. Shh," I said.

I went back to texting

Me:
Yeah. Sure. Who's driving? I am so not taking the bus.

Who am I? When did I learn to talk like this?

Charlene:
Mallory's brother.

Me:
But isn't he in college?

Charlene:
Nah. That's the other one. She has two. One in college and one sixteen.

Me:
How good is he at driving?

Charlene:
Might kill you, idk

Me:
Ha. You think you can get outta there?

Charlene:
Yeah. I got it.

I turned off my phone and raised my hand. Time for that acting camp to come in handy.

"Mr. Koffman? I don't feel so good …"

I pretended to act like I was about to throw up. It was convincing, if I do say so myself.

"She's gonna puke!" One of the boys in the class said.

I headed for the door with my bag and ran out. I knew the class well enough to know that one of Mr. Koffman's rules was if you're gonna throw up, you don't have to ask. I got into the hallways and met up with the girls.

"Hey guys," I said as I saw them coming into view.

"Hey. Glad you made it out. I heard Mr. Koffman is really tough,"

Charlene said.

"Oh, yeah. I know, right?" I replied.

I skipped math class. What was I doing? I loved math. I wanted to be an alternate, and I threw it all away with one fake move, didn't I?

"So, did you guys skip too?" I asked.

"I was in yearbook," Charlene commented.

"Doing online math," Mallory said. "Not a big deal to skip; I can catch up."

We all started walking to the front fast but quietly so no one could hear us. We were all silently giggling. I tried to giggle too, but I felt sick to my stomach. My hand brushed against my shorts by accident, and I felt something in my pocket. It was just a coin, but for a second, I thought it was the tin. I forgot I didn't bring it with me to school anymore, and the thought of it just made my stomach twist even more. The way nothing would be normal anymore, not after that.

We sneaked around the halls until we arrived at the front. A car horn beeped at us. We all spotted a forest-green Toyota Tundra.

"Get in," a brown-haired boy called to us.

Mallory turned to us and said, "He's the one."

We all got in, but we were silent the whole time. If we talked, it would probably end with a cringy comment from Mallory's brother.

We finally arrived at the mall, and we all hopped out, and Mallory's brother drove away. He would pick us up again in a few hours when the school day was over.

The car stopped in a parking lot, and the familiar storefront of the Bluewave Boutique wasn't too far away.

We walked towards the shop, looking at the displays of clothes in the windows on our way there. We were almost at the store when Charlene spotted a beautifully embroidered blouse on a display. She practically started drooling.

She rushed into the store to look for the blouse.

"I'll meet you guys at the cookie stand!" she yelled, not looking back.

"The cookie stand isn't part of the food court!" I yelled after her.

"Whatever!" She yelled back.

I rolled my eyes. All the time I spent learning references to impress Gwen—wasted.

I sighed. "I'm gonna go get Charlene," I said.

"I'll come with," Mallory replied.

We both walked into the store and understood why Charlene rushed in. It was a different kind of store than Nina's mom's boutique. There were more embroidered pieces and a ton of cute pieces like tweed waistcoats and vintage blouses.

Charlene spotted us, and she perked up. "Hey Mallory, I found these amazing shorts for you! So much better than those dirty gym ones."

She held up a pair of white shorts embroidered with teal leaves. Except they were *really* short. They would definitely show Mallory's cuts.

"Mmm …" I said. "I don't think they'd look really good on you, Mallory."

Mallory nodded at me. "Yeah. White isn't really my color."

"Hm … okay," Charlene said and put the shorts back.

Mallory looked at me and mouthed *thank you* when Charlene turned away.

When I got home with my bags of clothes, I snuck onto Mom and Dad's computer and erased the email that said I wasn't in class. I didn't know why, but I didn't feel bad about it. I felt empty. Just a bit. I put my backpack and my clothes in my room as I sat down on my bed. In my mind, it just wasn't a big deal. Maybe that was a problem, maybe I should have cared, but I just didn't. The more I thought about it, the more it scared me that I didn't seem to care.

I began to idly check my group chats until I saw a notification from the civics project group chat.

I opened it, reading the texts.

Ava:
Hey guys, do you think we could meet at the public library on Shell Street? The school library is closed right now, but I'm free if any of you guys can come.

Natalie:
Yeah, I could show up. We didn't have any homework today.

Nina:
Sure. I made some cool drawings to show you guys.

Me:
I can come

I sighed, walking over to Gwen's room. I didn't feel like talking to her, just in case she knew I skipped school, but I needed a ride.

I knocked on the door, opening it to reveal Gwen furiously typing on her computer for an essay. Or that's what I assumed it was. She usually typed on her bed when she wrote original stories like fanfic but only sat at her desk for schoolwork. She glanced over at me, taking off her headphones.

"Hey, Alex. How was school?" she asked.

"Fine. I need to go to the public library because my friends are doing a project there," I said. "It's for school. Can you please give me a ride?"

"Alright," she smiled, but it didn't reach her eyes.

My stomach churned. I really hoped she didn't know I skipped school. I didn't want to see that look of disappointment on her face that always made my stomach churn.

Gwen spent a few minutes packing up as I grabbed my purse and phone, quickly writing down a few ideas for the project to discuss. We got into the car, driving towards the library as Gwen put on *Shawshank* by the *Royston Club*.

"So, how was the cafe thing?" Gwen asked casually, driving forward.

"Well, Adrian got all the references which was a plus. It was super fun, actually," I said, smiling a bit.

"That's good. Y'know, my first date went awful," Gwen said.

"Gwen, you already told me this!" I laughed.

"When I was your age," Gwen mocked before shifting her tone to normal, "I met this guy. Pretty great, but the first date … well, it didn't fit. He barely knew any fandoms and didn't like anime-style art or any of my interests, so although he was cute, I had to let them go. So, I'm pretty glad that this guy isn't like that for you."

"Yeah," I smiled. "He's pretty great."

"That's good," Gwen smiled back.

I checked the project group chat to see where exactly we were meeting.

Natalie:
I'm here. You guys coming?

Me:
I'm on my way

I wasn't looking forward to seeing Natalie. This meeting was going to be so different than last week when she and I were worried about working with *The Pops*.

Ava:
Packing up my stuff. I'll be there in a few.

The library came into view after a few minutes. Gwen parked, and I got out of the car, saying a quick thank you on the way out.

I walked on the brick pathway towards the library, the glass doors sliding open for me. It was quiet inside, as usual, several pathways lined with bookshelves splitting off from the main room. Across the area, there were a few tables from where I could spot Natalie and Ava.

"Hey," I said, walking towards them. I put my stuff down as I sat next to Ava, across from Natalie. Natalie looked away as I sat down, her arms crossed.

"I'm here," Nina said quietly, racing towards the table with a sketchbook in her hands. "I'm sorry I was a little late. I forgot a detail on the map!"

"It's fine," Natalie said.

"Yeah, it's alright," I said.

Natalie glared at me, and I closed my mouth. Nina and Ava shared a look towards each other before Nina sat down.

"So," Ava said, pulling out a notebook. "I've organized a few of our ideas and did a bit of research over the weekend. I'll start, okay?"

Nina nodded, not entirely paying attention, as she continued drawing in her notebook.

"Alright, so I researched the term oligarchy to see if two people count. The only thing I got was a *small group of people*. Technically two people is a small group of people, so I think it counts."

"Mmm-hmm," Natalie said. "What about four people? Would that count?"

"Yep," Ava said. "Just a small group of powerful people count as an oligarchy."

"Then you and *The Pops* are part of an oligarchy, aren't you?" Natalie snapped. "But I guess it's five now, right?" She glared at me.

Everyone was quiet for a minute as Natalie locked eyes with me.

Ava cleared her throat. "Natalie, that's not how governments work," she said quietly. "Schools don't really have proper gover—"

"Alex, why aren't you saying anything? You're the one that ditched us, right?" Natalie spat.

"Natalie, calm down," Nina drawled, looking up from her drawing. "It's just a project."

"Just a project? Just a project! Nina, this isn't *about* the project!" Natalie said, raising her voice.

I turned a bit red. I should've seen this coming. My stomach churned. It was just going to be another fight, wasn't it? How could I be so stupid?

"Well then, what is it about?" Ava asked calmly.

I cringed in my head. That wasn't a good idea.

"It's about Alex!" Natalie yelled, getting a few shushes from the librarians. "You threw us away so you could be popular!"

"What are you talking about?" I replied.

Natalie rolled her eyes, beginning to raise her voice. "Oh, now you talk!"

"Natalie, you're being hysterical," Nina hissed. "We don't have time for a fight."

Natalie wasn't listening. "Alex, do you even watch *Tyrants* anymore? Or did your new friends find you something else to do?"

I opened my mouth to speak but couldn't really say anything. I had totally forgotten. That was our thing, but after I had nobody to share it with, I stopped watching.

Natalie pursed her lips. "You weren't in school today."

"Yeah, I was," I said.

This wasn't going to be good.

"Yeah. In the first period. But when science came along, I didn't see one glimpse of you."

"That's because I got sick in math," I lied.

Ava and Nina looked at each other nervously.

"Alex, you're awful at lying. Y'know I bet you skipped school," she said.

Silence.

Natalie stood up quickly, her chair roughly scraping the library's tile floor.

"I don't even know you anymore, do I?"

And with that, Natalie stormed out.

Ava and Nina looked at each other before speaking.

"Umm. Are you okay?" Ava said, pushing her papers aside and leaning in.

My head began to hurt. It was hard to think.

Nina moved her chair closer to me. "So, that's really random. Natalie dumped you as a friend? Why is she being mad and acting like you left her?"

"I don't know," my voice was quiet. "But, um, she's right about the skipping," I swallowed hard.

"I'll text Natalie later and coordinate our project," Ava offered. "That way, you don't have to talk to her right now. It seems like things need to cool off."

Nina nodded her head in agreement.

Keeping my head down, I said, "Thanks. A lot."

"So … let me show you the map that I did," Nina said, trying to change the subject. "I think you'll really like the detail of the shores."

I was thankful for the distraction, but my mind kept going back to what Natalie had said. Was I different? Why did I stop watching …

I really had changed, and that part started to eat at me. Was I really even the same person anymore? I didn't even know.

CHAPTER NINE – WEDNESDAY

My alarm blared, and I instinctively knocked it off the desk. I yawned, grabbing the rest of the papers strewn all over. I had never been up until 2am, not even for a sleepover. But there I was—I pulled my first semi-all-nighter by working on an essay. I organized the papers and put them in my folder, shoving them in my backpack. I picked out the new clothes I got from the day before and did the rest of my morning tasks. I finished breakfast and threw the rest of my heavy textbooks into my bag. I started walking out the door, and I pulled out my phone with its new galaxy phone case and started walking along the concrete.

Me:
Good morning

Adrian:
Hey :)

Me:
What r u doing?

Adrian:
On bus, sneaking an iced coffee

Me:
You tired?

Adrian:
A little. I don't drink coffee a lot, but today I was half asleep. But it didn't do a whole lot

Me:
Y so tired?

Adrian:
Math competition coming up. Needed to review exponent rules and attempted to learn something called matrix algebra.

Me:
Yeah the scalar multiplication can get really tricky

Adrian:
Wait what

I changed the subject. Charlene had told me not to be too smart. Guys don't like to feel threatened in a relationship.

Me:
Do you have *The Week* at your school?

Adrian:
Nah. But Red tells me all about it, so I have a pretty good idea of

what it is

Me:
Nice. I'm at a crosswalk. Bye

Adrian:
Bye :)

I didn't lie. I was sane enough to not text while crossing the road. I got to the other side, and then I could see the school coming into view. I opened The Pop's group chat. They had changed the image to be a red lollipop.

Me:
Hey pops!

Charlene:
Hey

Me:
Where are u?

Ava:
Behind you

I turned around. They were there alright. They caught up soon enough. Together, we walked to Homeroom, walking past the library.

"Oh. Be right back; I have to return a book," Mallory said, rushing into the library.

"Okay," Ava said as Mallory closed the door behind her.

I waited for a few seconds, picking at my nails, before I noticed Natalie reading a book inside the library.

My heart practically stopped. They were all still there, talking just like nothing was wrong. My stomach churned. Did they even need me to begin with? This all happened because of that stupid jelly bean. If I never took it, would we still be friends? Would I still be friends with anyone? What would have happened? Maybe this was better than the *what-ifs*, but it still seemed so wrong.

"Alright, I'm back!" Mallory said, walking back through the doors. "Let's go."

"Alright," Charlene said. "So, are you all excited for the trip tomorrow?"

.   .   .

I dashed into math, almost missing the bell. The problem of the day was displayed on the board.

When Mr. Koffman came to the front to explain the lame problem, I was finishing my text to Nina. I wasn't paying attention until he called on me.

"Uh … two?" I said.

It was a wild guess. It didn't really matter, though.

"That's incorrect," he said.

"Okay," I said, not paying any attention.

"What is going on with you?" Jay whispered.

"Yeah," Raaj said. "You literally skipped class yesterday."

"Hey, keep it down!" I whisper-yelled.

Raaj and Jay shared a concerned look and went back to taking notes. I looked up at the board. Quadratic equations. I tried to make sense of the FOIL method, but it seemed really complex. I must be really tired from not getting enough sleep last night. The rest of math I just texted. It wasn't a big deal. I didn't text Adrian; from what I knew, he wouldn't like me breaking the rules.

. . .

I shoved my books in my locker and checked my lipstick in my locker mirror. Nina had gifted me one.

"You never know when you need to make a good impression," she had said.

I closed the locker and jumped back when I saw a figure looming nearby.

"Omg. You scared me!" I yelped.

Thomas.

Thomas looked at me, quiet. He didn't say much of anything, but just the sight of him standing in front of me made my heart sink.

"What do you want?" I said coldly.

"I just wanted an answer, Alex," he said. "I don't know why you were so mad at me."

"Maybe because you left. And the others did as well," I snapped.

"No—" he said, sighing. "I mean, why did you say that stuff, to begin with. I don't know, you've just changed so much, and you even skipped school—"

I cut him off. "Oh, so now you're paying attention to me because I started to dress nice and wear lipstick? Y'know, I don't want to hear it, Thomas," I snapped. "Why don't you just go hang out with Perry? You like her better anyways."

"Alex, what are you—" Thomas said, confused.

"Just stop talking," I said harshly. "I'm done with this, and you, and all this stupid stuff that's happened. None of it matters anymore, so just leave me alone."

I slammed my locker door shut, striding past him.

"Alex!" he called after me, but I didn't care to respond.

It was over. He lost his chance, and it was over.

. . .

Although my friends distracted me with cute comments on *Instagram* during lunch, I couldn't shake the conversation with Thomas and the argument with Natalie.

Kids in the classroom began pulling out their homework as Mrs. Harlem walked around the class. I rolled my eyes and looked through my backpack. I couldn't find it. I couldn't find my homework. I looked through my backpack again. Then I realized. I didn't do it. The mall got me so preoccupied I didn't have time. Mrs. Harlem got to my desk.

"Homework?" she asked.

"I left it at home," I lied.

"Well, then you get a zero," she replied.

I'd never gotten a zero. I'd never even gotten a C. My heart started to pound. She started to go to the next desk when Ava came to my rescue.

"Wait. She did do it. I saw her doing it last night when we were all together and studying. She just forgot it. Nina can tell you."

"Nina?" Mrs. Harlem said, turning.

"Yeah. I saw her too. We all did. She explained the difference between meiosis and mitosis to us," Nina said straight-faced.

Mrs. Harlem looked at me sternly.

"Yeah. Two cells same, four cells different," I stammered.

"Hmmm … fine. Bring it tomorrow," Mrs. Harlem said.

I exhaled and pulled out my phone when Mrs. Harlem turned away.

Me:
Thank you so much

Ava:
No problem. That's what friends are for.

I looked at her before noticing Natalie beside me, rolling her eyes.

I shouldn't have cared, but I did.

. . .

When school was finished, Gwen drove me over to Charlene's house to get outfits for the field trip. I had been dodging Gwen most of this week, but I needed a ride. Again.

"So, Alex?" she said cautiously.

"Yeah," I asked dismissively, looking through the song list to distract myself. I casually looked through a few, reading the titles to some. "What about *Ghost* by *Confetti?*"

"Sure. Umm, I saw now you're wearing new clothes and stuff."

"So what?" I snapped.

"Hey," she said sternly. "Don't talk to me like that."

"Well, whatever," I said.

"Whoa. Whatever happened to the old Alex? Where's her old friends? Because I liked the old Alex a lot better."

"Well, the old Alex is gone! Right with her friends!" I yelled.

Gwen stopped the car at the yellow light.

"What?"

"My friends are being jerks, Gwen. Some stunt happened, and then they all left me! Now I have new friends, alright? This is really hard, so could you just quit it?"

"Alex, I didn't know—"

A car honked behind them. Gwen put her foot on the gas, taking the next turn.

"I don't want to talk about it. Her house is right there," I said, brushing her off.

I got out of the car before she had an excuse to stop me, walking to the door of the house.

Charlene's house was … normal. I was met with a small, short structured house with a white wood porch, freshly grown flowers flanking the edges. Given Charlene's bravado, I imagined she lived in a sprawling mansion.

It didn't scream popular. It just looked average. It was refreshing to see something so normal in so long.

Charlene opened the door to the house, waving as I walked up the driveway.

"Hey, girl!" she said, welcoming me in.

I noticed she didn't have any makeup on like she normally did. Usually, her face was covered in eyeshadow and lipstick, but she looked like she had just washed her face.

"Hey!" I responded, smiling. "Thanks for letting me over."

Charlene nodded. "Sure. My parents aren't home, so we have the place all to ourselves."

"That's perfect," I said, smiling as I walked inside.

"Do you want something to drink?" Charlene asked. "We have some lemonade and iced tea in the fridge."

"Iced tea is fine," I said, smiling as I followed her into the kitchen. Charlene pulled out a large jug of sweet tea, beginning to pour me a glass. She got a cup of lemonade for herself.

"So, how was the date with Adrian?" Charlene asked as she poured the sweet-smelling drink into the glass.

"Really good," I said, grabbing my cup. "Thanks for the tea." I sipped a bit as I continued. "It was a really good time, and I think it'll probably work."

"That's great," Charlene smiled, sipping the lemonade. "Alright. Let's head to my room. Just don't spill the drinks."

I followed Charlene to her room as I drank more of the sweet-flavored tea.

Her room looked casual with its sky-blue walls and lavender bed and blanket. A few assorted stuffed animals were placed neatly around the room. She had a desk with some homework on it, some shelves to store her belongings, and some boxes stored underneath the desk.

On the side of her room was the main attraction … a walk-in closet with clothes hung neatly inside.

"Thanks for letting me come over to borrow stuff. All the new clothes are too nice to wear to the theme park. And if I go to one more clothing store, my parents will ground me for spending so much."

"Not a problem," Charlene replied. "I'd do anything for an excuse to pick out clothes," Charlene grinned as she filed through her closet.

"What about this one?" I said, holding up a white blouse with navy blue jeans.

"No white. It'll get grimy," she said.

"Smart." I put it back and found another one. "How's this?" I said, holding a light gray t-shirt with little embroidered blue and green flowers on it.

"Nah," she said, wrinkling her nose. "Maybe this?" Charlene asked, grabbing a patterned shirt.

"It looks nice, but it's long-sleeved," I said. "It'll be pretty hot."

Charlene nodded, putting it back. "Makes sense."

"Hey, what about this one?" I held up a lightweight pink cardigan and a matching yellow one. "We could wear these with T-shirts underneath," I said.

"Ooh, that's good," Charlene said. "I also have matching skirts with that set, and there's jean shorts that work as well if we aren't up for that."

"That's perfect," I said. "Well, now that we're done, why don't we just look for fun? You have the best clothes," I added.

"Uh ... sure. And thank you," she said. "Ew. I don't like this song. Let me pick a different Spotify playlist."

I saw a jean jacket nestled between two shirts and pulled it out.

"This is amazing quality. The detailing is awesome. Where did you get this?" I asked, coming out of the closet.

"I'm not sure," she said, still focused on her laptop.

I checked the tag. There wasn't one.

"It says … *made with love*?" I read.

Charlene's face snapped up from the laptop. Her eyes went wild as she froze in her spot.

She stormed over to me. "Give me that. You weren't supposed to see that," she said, panicked, taking it from my hand. "And don't look in my closet again," she snapped.

I took a step back. "Charlene, what does that mean?" I gestured to the pretty jacket. "And why are you freaked out?" I asked.

"It's nothing. Just forget it."

I crossed my arms, looking at her critically. "It certainly doesn't seem like nothing. You're starting to hyperventilate."

Charlene tried to rip the tag off the jacket. She gave up and shoved the jacket back into the closet.

"Just drop it!" Tears started to appear in her eyes.

I lowered my arms and softened my voice. "Charlene, what's going on? I'm not going to hurt you. Just tell me."

She wiped her eyes with her hand.

"Do you promise not to tell?" she sniffled.

"I swear," I replied.

She took a deep breath.

"I'm a fraud!" she blurted out. "I don't really have any money, and I'm a horrible friend because I make Nina buy my clothes and—"

"Whoa, Charlene, slow down! What does this have to do with the jacket?" I asked carefully.

"I made it," she said, wiping away a tear on her face. "I sewed it because I can't buy that many clothes, and grandma had the stuff—"

"What?" I blinked. "You did all this yourself? Or just the detailing? Wait, oh my, did you sew all this from scratch? Charlene, that's amazing!"

"It's not that cool," Charlene said through her tears. "And yeah, I made all of it—"

"Of course, it is. I can barely sew on a button. So slow down; what's wrong?"

"I'll explain," she said, motioning to sit down on her bed. "When I was a kid, I was taken away from my parents because they were unstable. My dad was abusive, and my mom lost it," Charlene sniffled.

"Charlene, I'm so sorry."

Charlene nodded, continuing, "I went to live with my grandma for a few years, and she taught me how to sew. I got really good at it."

She walked over to the bedside table, taking a tissue from the box, and blowing her nose. She slumped down into her bed before continuing.

"My grandmother said my great-grandfather was a tailor, and he would be really proud of me." She paused, taking in a breath. "My mom put her life together, but my grandmother is still my guardian. My mom is allowed to live with us. My father … well, he's not allowed to be around us. My mom works, but we don't have money to spend on clothes. I can buy fabric and make my own. I never told anyone." Tears welled up in her eyes.

I sat down next to her on the bed. "You don't get to see your dad? Ever?"

She grabbed another tissue and wiped her nose.

"No. And after the way he hurt my mom, I don't ever want to see him anyway."

"And you have to live with your grandmother?"

"Yeah. It's something about how the courts work. You only have a certain amount of time to be stable or get a job. I guess my mom wasn't on their timeline," she said dolefully.

"And the clothes …"

"Yeah. When I outgrow the clothes that are name brands, I remove the label and resew them into my clothes," she explained. "Also, um … do you remember last year when you complimented me on my outfit?"

"Yeah," I said, looking at her.

I remembered that day. It was not a good memory.

"I sewed that outfit, and I, um, I really wanted to thank you because I hadn't done that type of stitching before and was really proud of it. But I got anxious that someone would realize I sewed it, so I was rude to you so no one else would ask me about it," Charlene trailed off. "What I meant to say was that I was super sorry for snapping at you. After that, I got really nervous, and I didn't wear that outfit again. So now I guess it was a good time to tell you."

I let this new information sink in.

"It was a really good outfit, Charlene. I know you have to keep up the act, but you're good at sewing. It's really cool."

Charlene looked up, her eyes still wet. "Thanks."

A long pause.

"The other *Pops* don't know. Do they?"

Charlene shook her head. "It would bring up too many questions. I think Mallory suspects. But I didn't want to be the weird kid who sews her own clothes. No matter how nice they may look."

"Why tell me?"

Another long pause. She raised her face and finally looked into my eyes. "Because last week you were the weird kid. And you know how much that sucks. You are the only one who would understand why I lied."

Charlene was right. I did.

We sat quietly for a while, and then she added, "I'm the bossy fashionable one in the group, and I'm a fake. And the one thing I'm really good at, I have to hide."

Charlene grabbed a small giraffe from her bed and held it close to her chest.

I tried to make eye contact, but Charlene continued to look down.

"I understand why you don't want to tell anyone. But you have real talent." Charlene finally looked up. She looked so young with no makeup and her face wet with tears.

"You should start entering contests or something. Do a middle school *Project Runway* club. Make it cool," I suggested.

She sniffled. "Yeah, I guess you have a point," she said, but I knew she wasn't ready to make a change like that.

After a while, I left.

That night, I started thinking. Everyone has something. And everyone is afraid they will be alone because of it.

CHAPTER TEN – THURSDAY

Today was the field trip. I put on the yellow cardigan Charlene let me borrow. Before I left yesterday, she showed me some of the detailing she did, and now I know the importance of always checking for a French seam. I was still a little shaken up about the secrets I had heard. Did my old friends have secrets too? My secret used to be that I was awkward. Now my secret was that I wasn't awkward. Well, it wasn't really a secret. The true secret was the jelly bean and that I had cheated my way into being *normal*. My phone pinged, and I could see my friends were already arriving at the school. I grabbed a small purse and slipped on my shoes before dashing out the door. I didn't say bye to Gwen; it would just take more time.

I rushed to school so I wouldn't be late. I speed walked; if I ran,

I would probably fall on the concrete; and if I fell, I probably wouldn't be able to go on the field trip. Soon enough, I saw the school up ahead, and the buses were pulling in. They were the nice buses with movies in them, air conditioning, and most importantly, Wi-Fi and outlets for charging. I went into the school cafeteria so the teachers would tell me where to go. Everyone was chattering excitedly, and some people were heading for the bathrooms because the teachers were telling us to not use the bathrooms on the bus unless it was an emergency. Something about how it would make the bus smell all day.

Soon enough, our teachers called us to board the bus. I was on the bus with *The Pops*, so I got to sit with them. I was on bus G, a name tag on my shirt with the text written in forest green. The bus was whirring as gas clouded the air. The school was still a little dark since it was only six in the morning. Although huge, there were only two people per seat, so Charlene sat with Josh. I sat with Nina on my side and Ava and Mallory on the other. The ride was two hours, so we kept ourselves busy with the movie they picked out. It was a long drive, but the bus was nice enough to keep us from going insane. They had a navy-blue carpet on the bottom with some colorful triangles decorating it. The same pattern was also used for the seats. The bus had huge windows, and luckily, the glass wasn't tinted an ugly yellow. The bus started moving, and the chatter immediately picked up. They put on a movie. It seemed like it was about a bunch of kids playing baseball in a dirt lot. And something about a large dog, but I wasn't paying much attention.

I pulled out my sparkling light blue phone and a pair of earbuds.

"Hey, do you have any good music on there?" Nina asked.

"Sure," I said, handing her one of my earbuds.

She placed it in her ear, and I scrolled through my Spotify.

"Ooh, what are all those playlists?" she said curiously.

I could feel my palms beginning to sweat.

"Oh, sorry. I just make a lot of playlists. I make playlists for songs that remind me of certain characters. It's really weird, I know."

Her face lit up. "No, it's not! That's really cool. I actually know some of these characters," she said, beaming.

"Oh really?" I asked. "Which ones?"

"I've heard of Whitney Crowne. I also know Mayor Story, as well as Matt and Belle."

"Ooh, that's so cool! So you've watched *Tyrants*?" I asked.

"Not a ton," Nina admitted. "But Red watches a few of the streamers, and I love drawing the landscapes in the bases."

"Ah. That's pretty cool! So which playlist do you want me to play?"

She thought for a minute. "How about the *Summer Days* playlist? I know we're not in summer, but I really like that stuff."

"Oh, definitely!" I said, clicking the playlist.

The song *Heat Waves* started playing.

We were both mouthing the lyrics, and then an ad flipped on. Nina turned towards me.

"I love that song. You have some pretty good taste!" she said, beaming. "Also, did you make that cover art yourself? I really like it."

"Oh, I did. I made it using Adobe Photoshop. It took me a while, but I think it was worth it."

"It totally was. It looks low-key awesome."

I was about to respond when my phone buzzed. I pulled the phone towards me.

"Sorry. Someone's texting me," I said, pausing the next song.

I inhale.

Angel.

Angel:
Hey Alex. I miss you. Do you think we could talk?

I felt a pang in my heart. She was probably sitting alone on a bus, and that's why she texted. She was just like Thomas. She only wanted to talk to me because I had some social credit. I balled up my fist.

Angel didn't care at all what I thought previously, and now she had the audacity to text me. She left me on read for almost a week without saying a word. It was far too late to ask for apologies now.

"Hey, is something wrong?" Nina asked.

"No. No, it's fine," I said, swiping the text closed and queuing the next song.

Nina made some suggestions for songs, and I added them to my playlist. But my mind kept coming back to the text from Angel. About an hour later, we finally arrived at Animal Park.

As we pulled in, Mallory yawned. "I'm so tired," she said. "That ride was painfully long."

Charlene and Josh came up behind us, holding hands.

"It was only two hours," Josh commented. "I don't understand why that's so tiring."

Charlene nudged his shoulder, but she had a playful look on her face. I only knew Josh from PE. There were whisperings around the school that Josh had a thing for Charlene, and I could see why. Besides the fact she was the most popular girl in school, they were good friends beforehand. At least from what I had heard.

Before we could take off, Mrs. Harlem stopped us. "Be back by 4:45 sharp!" she announced.

Josh tugged on Charlene's hand, "C'mon! Let's get to the Serpent," he said, a goofy grin stretching across his freckle-dotted face.

We were all running fast, but the lines were long. The sign said it was a thirty-five-minute wait. I was still panting when we got into the line. I leaned against the nearby decorative coral, my hands on my knees as I tried to catch my breath when I heard a familiar voice.

"The download took forever last night. Given all the Nooks, you think it would be faster," Thomas complained.

I froze, slowly looking up. My heart slowed down when I realized he was talking to Natalie. There were a few people in front of us, but we could hear them anyway.

I turned to Nina. "Hey, have you all tried the new *Animal Crossing* update?" I asked her.

Josh turned suddenly and started to gush. "Yeah! It's so cool! I love the Nook miles tickets, and you can go to other islands to raid them! I really like the museum! It's so cool! Have you gotten an art wing yet? Because you can get the paintings from Jolly Redd, and he can sell you fa—"

Nina cut him off. "Ugh. We are not going to sit in line talking about kid's games."

Josh slunk back in shame. I gave him a shrug and a sad smile. I was disappointed at Nina shutting down the conversation. At least I could be who I wanted to be with my old friends. Now I had to be something I wasn't. We sat down on the benches for a late lunch before we got back on the bus. Charlene had brought out extra chips for everyone, and Ava shared her popcorn and pulled out the photos she bought on the Serpent ride.

"Omg. We look ridiculous! Mallory, your face looks terrified!" Ava giggled.

"Give that to me," Mallory said before she yanked the photo out of her hand.

She really did look terrified.

I leaned over her shoulder to get a better look.

"Whoa, we both look scared! Check out my eyes!" I said to help her feel not so alone.

Charlene and Nina were posing as if it was a modeling contest.

Mallory gave me a shy smile. "Yeah, you can certainly tell that we were on a roller coaster. Which I guess is the point of the photos," she said, casting a sidelong glance at Charlene.

"Oh, don't be such a sore loser just because Nina and I knew when to smile," Charlene said before taking a bite into her turkey sandwich.

Nina chuckled, stabbing a fork into her salad.

"Yeah. Charlene and I came here last summer, and we rode that ride five times until we figured out when to smile. Those photos were atrocious!" she said, popping an olive in her mouth.

Mallory finally relented and smiled. Sometimes they were mean to each other, but sometimes they helped each other feel good about themselves. *The Pops* were complicated like that.

After finishing up our lunches and tossing items correctly into the garbage and recycling bins, Ava exclaimed, "Hey! I absolutely want a churro." Everyone agreed, even Nina, who had been saying no to junk food all day.

I almost burned my hand on the fried dough, the smell of cinnamon and sugar creating a cloud around us.

"Yum! This is delicious," Nina exclaimed, biting into the caramel-colored treat. "I had no idea this even existed."

Charlene and Mallory chuckled and dared her to eat a second one.

"You don't have to dare me. I am totally eating another one."

Charlene took out her phone and took some shots of Nina enjoying her sugar snack.

My phone alarm went off, letting me know we needed to head back to the buses. We started walking back to the bus and began to steer towards a bathroom. We saw Mrs. Harlem waving at us.

"Girls! Where were you? The buses are waiting for you. You were supposed to be back fifteen minutes ago."

I glanced at my alarm, and it said 4:32. We weren't due back at the buses until 4:45.

"We are on time," I protested.

Mrs. Harlem held out her watch. It read 5:03.

My breathing began to become shallow. I looked at my phone, and it clicked over to 4:33. I breathed deeply.

"Shoot. I must have messed up the time somehow."

No big. The buses weren't going to leave without the popular girls.

Mrs. Harlem just sighed and told us to get on the buses.

Nina stood rooted to the spot.

"Nina. Come on," Ava said, looking over her shoulder.

Nina began to step backward. "No, I have to use the bathroom. I'll just be a minute."

Mrs. Harlem walked back, trying to grab her arm. "Nina. You are late. You can use the bathroom on the bus. We need to go."

Nina yanked her arm away before Mrs. Harlem could touch her. She began shaking her head side to side, and began to become ashen.

"No … no. I can't."

Charlene began to giggle. "Seriously, Nina, the bathroom on the bus is gross. But not that gross. Come on."

I noticed Nina's breathing becoming shallower, and she began to tremble. I've never had a panic attack, but I've felt my chest tightening before. Nina looked worse.

"Mrs. Harlem," I started. "This is totally my fault for being late. But Nina was saying she wasn't feeling well earlier. And it's best she uses this bathroom. Right. Now."

I didn't wait for an answer. I just ran at Nina and tore off to the bathroom with her. I caught a glimpse of Mrs. Harlem's reddening face before the door to the bathroom shut.

Nina burst into a stall and threw herself in front of the toilet. She shoved her finger down her throat and started to dry heave.

"Nina …" I said gently, "I don't know if you have to throw up. It looks like you were just upset. Maybe the heat."

She continued to put her finger down her throat until I heard the vomiting. I looked away at the noise, feeling myself start to get nauseated.

Between the heaving, she said, "You are so … stupid. How did you mess up your clock?"

More vomiting.

"No one messes up a phone clock. I couldn't even find a single-stall bathroom, thanks to *you*."

The vomiting stopped, and I tried to help her up.

Nina pulled away, spitting out, "No, I haven't reached the bottom. I ate a red *Twizzler* when we got here."

I took a step back, letting this sink in. Reach the bottom? The day's events ran through me: Nina refusing to eat snacks. Always refusing to eat snacks. How she lingered in the bathroom after every lunch period. Always eating gum after lunch. The panic about not being able to use the bathroom right now. And memorizing a colored food to know when she vomited it up.

"You're bulimic," I sputtered.

Nina looked up, her face paler than before.

"None of the others know," she said, her eyes pleading. "Or they don't care."

"I won't say anything, and I'm sure they would care. But we need to talk about this later. Let me help you get cleaned up."

This time, she did let me help her and even put her weight on my shoulder as we walked out of the bathroom.

.   .   .

We were all tired. The sun would set by the time we got back. Nina explained everything to me when we got on.

"Nina, are you okay?" I asked, just making sure.

"Hey, whisper, okay? I know everyone's wearing earbuds, but this is embarrassing," she said.

"Alright," I replied, lowering my voice. "So, are you alright?"

"Yeah," she said. "The only reason I do this is because of my mom."

"She makes you throw up?" I asked with a frown.

"No. I would call you stupid, but I've never told anyone, so you wouldn't know."

She continued, "Look, my mom was a model, and she got fired because she was *too fat*. So my mom always wanted me to follow in her footsteps and be a model too. But I didn't want to be a model. I didn't have a choice." She paused, closing her eyes to compose herself. "She was always monitoring my weight and telling me to stop eating certain things. Thanksgiving is a disaster in my home. My grandparents make all these comments about my mom's weight. And occasionally, my dad does also."

Nina stopped talking. I put my hand on hers, silently wanting her to know that I was there for her.

She continued, "One night, I saw her vomiting in her bathroom, and I was able to figure it out. And soon enough, I started purging, also. I probably wouldn't be fat that way, so that's why."

I was speechless. I was gonna be making a lot of trips to the guidance counselor.

We sat in silence for the rest of the ride, just watching the movie. I continued to stroke the back of her hand with my thumb. Sometimes she wiped silent tears away with her other hand. But she never pulled away from me. Coach Hill got sick of the new films, and he put *Princess Bride* on. A bunch of students groaned, but I could see them quoting some parts silently.

As we were getting off the bus, Ava found me so her parents could check me out. It was too late for the school to let us walk home. Both my parents and Gwen were busy until later, so I planned to spend some time at Ava's until Gwen was done with her study group.

Ava's house was two stories tall, painted a fresh white with clean black shingles lacing the rooftop. Round bushes decorated the outside of the house, dotted with purple and pink flowers, although a few petals and leaves had begun to brown on the edges. Ava's room was on the second story, with a small round window to show her outside. There was a huge bookcase stretching across the right-hand wall, which was where the entrance was.

"Hey, I need to tell you something," Ava said, plopping down on her lavender-colored bed.

Oh no. Here we go again.

"Um. Should I sit down for this?"

Ava looked at me quizzically. "Sure?"

I sat down on the fluffy yellow ottoman, making myself comfortable for another huge self-disclosure.

"Okay. I'm ready."

"Remember last Friday when Charlene got back at you?"

"Yeah," I replied.

Ava rushed her words as if she had to get them out before she changed her mind. "Charlene was pissed at you on Wednesday for standing up for yourself. I don't think I've ever seen her so mad. So, she called Perry and Brit and told them to give you the dare on Thursday. Charlene eventually saw Perry and Brit weren't up for the task, so we did it ourselves. Mallory made the recording from what you said on Thursday." Ava looked ashamed.

My eyebrows raised all the way to my hairline. The people who I have spent all week in, who took me in, are the ones who …

I realized I was still in the room with Ava, who was waiting for me to respond. To yell? Did I feel like yelling? I was dumbfounded. Why would she tell me this? The people I had trusted all week had been lying. When I thought about it, I wasn't surprised by what they did, but still … I thought they cared about me. But in reality, they just ruined my life.

"How did you know all this?" I asked.

Ava started to bite her nail. "She made the call at my house. I heard everything."

"Why tell me now?"

She looked down at the carpet. She kept rubbing her foot back and forth on the floor as if she was trying to make static electricity.

"Because it was a crappy thing to do. And she decided it was okay to manipulate it so your other friends would hate you and you would be alone. People shouldn't do that. And I'm sorry I was a part of it."

My mouth popped open.

She went on, "I'm glad that we are friends now. I really wish that I had talked to you last year when we were in band together. You're really kind and care about your friends. I don't know why your other friends gave you up so easily. I mean … saying something mean about someone can be a big deal, but for them all to abandon you that way is crappy."

There was an ache in my chest when I thought about them. But Ava was right. I don't know why they gave up so easily. People that I barely knew were trusting me, but friends I had known most of my life wouldn't even listen to my side of things. Things were so messed up.

I knew the jelly bean was improving my social skills, but the jelly bean also changed people's perceptions of me. Was it also somehow affecting other people, so they trusted me faster?

I kept thinking about this even after I had brushed my teeth and was trying to fall asleep in my bed. Would I have been friends with *The Pops* if we had met earlier? Would my old friends like me with the jelly bean? Would anyone like me without it?

CHAPTER ELEVEN – FRIDAY

Nina pulled out her books for first period and closed her locker.

"So, did you hear that some of the boys are going to the dance in a huge group so they can just stockpile a ton of snacks?" she asked.

"I heard something like that," Ava said. "A little impressive if you ask me."

"So, does everyone have their outfits?" Charlene asked. "I picked mine a few days ago."

"Yep," Mallory said. "I'm so excited."

"Agreed," I said.

"Hey Mallory, you got a sec?" I asked.

"Sure." She turned to Charlene and Nina, "We'll catch up." She turned back to me. "What's up?"

"I think you need to go to the guidance counselor," I said.

"No, I don't," she replied immediately.

"You do. Mallory, I think that'll be good for you," I said.

"But my parents won't pay for therapy," she said.

"But the guidance counselor is free."

"But what if that goes on my record," Mallory rambled. "What if they tell someone? I can't risk that!"

"Mallory," I said calmly. "Promise me, the counselors don't spill personal information. I think you should look for help, even if they do tell someone."

"I don't need help!" she exclaimed, striding off.

I sighed. I needed to have the same conversation with Nina. I hoped that one went better.

·   ·   ·

I slumped over in my seat and started to put my books away. I didn't understand what Mr. Koffman was saying. Everyone had bad days, I tried to tell myself. As I stood up, Raaj and Jay were waiting to talk to me.

"What's going on, Alex? Are you okay?" Raaj said, looking irritated and concerned at the same time.

"It's nothing," I said, trying to walk past them.

Jay moved to block me as we exited the classroom. "No, really. What's going on?"

I looked around in the hallway for some of *The Pops*. Maybe they could rescue me from this conversation?

Raaj's voice snapped me back to attention. "Alex, last week you were super smart and funny. Now you are wearing lipstick, and you're acting like you're bad at math. What's going on?"

"Last week, I wasn't funny," I snapped. "Last week, I was weird and gawky."

"Alex, what are you saying? You're fine how you are," Jay said, baffled.

"Yeah, you might have been a little weird at some points, but you were still good!" Raaj tried.

"Wow, that helps a lot," I scoffed.

Jay glared at Raaj.

"That's um—not what we were saying. You're *our type* of weird. You'll see when you go to a competition." Jay continued, "We put your name down at the beginning of the year to try out for the math team, but you didn't show up."

"Yeah," Raaj said. "Did we freak you out when we brought up being an alternate?"

I opened my mouth to respond, but the bell rang, cutting me off.

They signed me up?

.   .   .

A few hours later, in Mrs. Harlem's class, we did a lab with colored water. We were all separated into groups, and I was working with Ava, who accidentally knocked over a beaker with water, spilling it across the table.

"Oh shoot, I'm so sorry!" Ava said, beginning to get up.

Some of the red dye spilled across my shirt as I got up.

"Mrs. Harlem, can we go to the bathroom?" Ava asked.

"Fine," she said. "Just clean up the water, please."

After a few minutes of cleaning up the mess, we walked to the bathroom.

"Mrs. Harlem is so boring," I complained, walking into the bathroom.

I stepped into the stall, waiting for Ava to reply.

"I know, right?" she said. "We already learned all of this. Honestly, I just use Mallory's notes to get through tests. I love good grades, but I'm not really learning anything new."

"That makes sense. Mallory takes notes on everything, right?" I asked.

"Most things," Ava said. "There was one class she got so bored she didn't take any notes at all."

"Really?" I asked, shocked.

"Yep," Ava laughed. "She fell asleep right in class!"

"Ha!" I laughed. "So what, was this in sixth grade?"

"Third," she said. "We went to elementary school together. She was the one that actually got me in the group in the first place. I mean, I'm the only one without a title. Charlene's the leader, Nina's pretty, Mallory's smart, and I'm just there, y'know?"

"No, don't say that," I said, flushing the toilet. "You're really great. Out of all of them, you're probably the nicest."

"But you don't really get an award for being nice, do you?" Ava sighed, washing her hands.

She set her phone on the sink counter to make sure no water spilled on it.

I put some soap on my hands as I began to run the water. It was quiet between the two of us for a few seconds before the silence was cut by a buzz from Ava's phone.

I saw the name pop up on the screen immediately.

Angel?

Angel:
Miss you. Can't wait to see you tonight. Wish we could go to the dance together :(

Ava grabbed her phone, wet hands and all.

"Ava?" I asked, looking at her, my eyes wide.

Ava's face was red as she tucked her phone behind her back.

"What?"

"Are you … dating Angel?"

"No," she said immediately, blushing. "You weren't supposed to see that."

"Why?" I asked.

"Because my parents don't like gay people, and you're gonna tell them, and then I'm gonna end up just like my aunt," she said, words pouring out of her mouth too fast for her to control.

"Wait. What do you mean?" I asked.

"My aunt is a lesbian, and my parents refuse to speak to her, and I have to have a separate social media account just to talk with her. And I don't wanna be kicked out of the house with nowhere to go," she said, tears filling her eyes and her voice starting to crack.

I just stood there, eyes wide with soap still on my hands.

"You already know my parents don't like gay people, so just, please don't tell," she begged.

"I swear. I've gotten really good at keeping secrets."

So good.

Tears welled up in her eyes, and I continued, "Ava. You should be allowed to like who you want. This is yours to tell or not tell. I saw nothing."

Ava exhaled slightly. "It's just—it's been hard. I already had the girls trying to set me up with Josh's cousin, and then Angel had to watch that. And I'm worried about her, Alex," she said, brushing tears out of her eyes.

"Why are you worried?" I asked. "Is something wrong?"

Ava looked to the side. "I think this … our relationship … has been hard on her. I don't think she likes herself as much as she used to. I'm trying to tell her that she's amazing, but I don't feel like it's coming through."

I didn't know what to think. Angel was my best friend a week ago. Did she not trust me with knowing that? Had I just not noticed? I was happy for both of them, but I wasn't sure how to feel about it. Did I do something wrong?

Ava blew her nose on the crummy brown paper towels.

"So, Alex," Ava said, switching the subject, "we're getting together for the group project again after school. We're just doing it at the library today. Are you free?"

"Yeah," I said, "sounds good."

We walked back to class, now with another thing swirling around in my head.

.   .   .

A few hours later, the last bell of the day rang. I sighed as I packed up the supplies I used in writing class. Natalie gathered her things as well, and we walked to the library in silence. We hadn't talked since she emotionally vomited on me at the last meeting. We distanced ourselves as we walked towards the library, seeing Ava sitting at a table near the back.

I sat at the table, trying not to pay attention to Natalie.

"Hey Ava, how's it going?" I asked.

"Good," Ava replied. "I wasn't able to do a ton of research because I got busy."

"Okay," Natalie said. "I didn't do a lot of work either. Where's Nina? Could she not make it?"

As if on cue, the door burst open, revealing Nina holding several folders and a sketchbook, with her phone sandwiched between them. The librarian shushed her, and I saw Nina mouth *sorry* to her.

"Hey guys, sorry I'm late!" Nina said, sitting at the table as she dropped the pile down on the table. "I made a few things for you guys. Last meeting was pretty unproductive, so I wanted to make sure we had everything we needed."

Nina grabbed the folders, passing one to each of us.

"I made us all folders specifically for the project, so we don't lose anything. I put a document inside that has all the current research on our society and all our plans as of now."

"Oh my, Nina, when did you do this?" Natalie asked, her eyes wide.

I was also surprised. The last few meetings, Nina had been inattentive, only chiming in every now and then.

"Over this week. I'm usually not too busy, but my mom says I always have to get good grades or I can't go on dates. And Red and I want to go to the botanical gardens, but my grades are slipping, so I decided we have to blow this project out of the park," she said, organizing the rest of her items.

I started to flip through the folder.

"This is so cool," I said. "Thank you so much for doing this."

"Yeah," Nina said. "I wanted to make sure everything was organized and ready to go so we could get straight into it. So does anyone have any new developments?"

There was no response.

"Just me?" Nina asked. "Alright then, so here are some things I did."

Nina opened her sketchbook, showing several drawings of the land. There was a sketch of a floating botanical garden, as well as a more land-based version. A map was cleanly drawn out on the side, with labels for each location.

We all leaned in, admiring her work.

"This is awesome," Natalie said.

"Oh yeah! And I designed a flag!" Nina said excitedly, opening her phone.

She showed us an image of a colored X across a white background, each leg of the X a different color.

"I based it off the colors of the seasons. I made some other versions as well with just two colors since we're doing a two-person oligarchy."

"This is super impressive," Ava said, looking through the folder. "I always love it when you go all out on this kind of stuff. Definitely not to be underestimated."

"Yep," Nina grinned. "So, where should we start?"

I glanced over at Natalie, still unsure if we were going to be able to work together.

I said tentatively, "Maybe we should start with rules," I said. "It's the main part, but we still haven't done anything."

"We could base it off the Bill of Rights and Constitution," Ava said.

"But that's already been done. We could summarize some points of the Constitution and then just write more interesting rules. Personally, I don't want to plagiarize anything. We'd get marked down so much if we tried that," Natalie said.

We all nodded, and Ava suggested, "I think it can be summarized down to freedom of speech, no unreasonable searches, protection of the accused, and no infringement of rights. We could go into more detail, but those are the main parts. The others were more situational laws, like the third amendment. People aren't exactly keeping soldiers in their houses these days."

"Alright, that seems doable," Natalie said. "But what else should we include?"

She glanced at me but looked down when I didn't look away. Natalie was vicious to me the last two times we spoke. First, to wrongly attack me about Thomas and then at the meeting. I was still hurt.

"Personally, I think there should be some strict equality laws.

Prejudice, discrimination, and other things will be illegal. Everyone should be given equal opportunities," Ava said.

"Agreed," Nina said. "It would be nice to start a country without a history of racism and colonialism."

"Or sexism," Natalie said. "Equal pay should be granted under law."

"That sounds good." I added, "People should also be granted a place of residence under our constitution as well. Homelessness is a big problem, so having some sort of law to counteract that is important."

"Ooh, and I could design group homes or small apartment complexes so that there's enough room for everyone," Nina said excitedly. "If this is entirely fictional, we could have floating buildings and stuff! That'd be so fun to draw."

"I don't think Mrs. Esma said anything against futuristic technology, so go ahead," Ava said.

Natalie cleared her throat. "Umm. I'm sorry for what I did at our last meeting."

I sat quietly, with my mouth pinched.

Ava looked between the two of us before speaking. "That's okay. We are on track now, and we'll get this all done next week. The presentation isn't for a while."

I continued to stare at Natalie, knowing she was really talking about us. Did I want to be friends with Natalie again? Did she want to be friends with the new me? My head hurt.

Natalie broke the silence, "Alex, I really—"

"I can't do this now."

I stood up, looking over at Nina. "This was so amazing. Thank you for getting us back on track."

I was going to be mature and walk out. But then I saw Natalie roll her eyes.

I slammed my books down on the desk and said sharply to Natalie, "You don't get to judge me when you dumped me."

Nope, maturity gone.

"You dumped Thomas first. That was humiliating to him!" she whisper-shouted.

"I did not. That was—"

I stopped and looked at Ava, her eyes wide. I was going to say that it was *The Pops* who set me up. Eight years I had been friends with Natalie, Angel, and Thomas, and they let it fall apart on a rumor and a poorly edited voice recording.

I looked back at Natalie. "It doesn't matter. You never bothered to ask me what really happened because you didn't care to ask."

Then I felt myself get heated, not caring who heard. "We used to make fun of *The Pops* by saying they all had to act a particular way and be perfect. That they would probably get kicked out of the group if they didn't follow

Charlene's rules." I heard Nina gasp, but I kept going leaning across the table to put my face near Natalie. "But you are the same as them. I didn't act the way you wanted, and rather than talk to me, you ghosted me and blocked me so I couldn't explain."

The librarian shushed me, and I breathed to calm down. "Look, we will work together, but we aren't friends because you didn't believe in me."

I turned away and walked towards the door before she could see my tears.

. . .

I closed my computer. When I came home, I had crawled into my bed with my laptop and watched *YouTube* videos for at least two hours. Gwen had knocked on the door asking if I wanted chocolate chip cookies, but I lied and told her I had a bad headache. It had only been a week, but everything felt big. Some parts were a mess, and other parts were really good. I saw the text from Charlene and opened it.

Charlene:
What are you wearing for the dance tomorrow?

Me:
Light blue dress. Long, swoopy, spaghetti strap. It's one of those layer dresses where you have the colored layer, and then you have a clear fabric layer with designs on it.

Charlene:
Oooh. Good one

I didn't text for a few seconds. I didn't really know what to say.

Charlene:
So... Do you like it? Is it pretty?

Me:
Well... yeah, of course, it's pretty, it wouldn't be ugly, right?

Charlene:
Um... yeah

Me:
So what are you wearing?

Charlene:
Dusty rose long sleeve for top of dress, and the bottom is light gray with pink orchids on it. Bottom longer in the back than front

Me:
Did you make it yourself?

Charlene:
No, my grandma drove me to this adorable vintage shop in Orlando a month ago and I found it there

Me:
So...

Charlene:
What?

Me:
Uh... I forgot. Gotta go. Cya!

It was wearing off. Right when I needed it.

CHAPTER TWELVE – SATURDAY

I was awkward again.

I had spent the morning on *Instagram* looking at ways to reduce anxiety, hoping it would help with my social skills. So far, I had done box breathing, somatic grounding, and went for a long walk while listening to dolphin noises. Now I was super relaxed but still awkward.

I glanced at the clock. It was 4:00. The dance wouldn't be until 6:00, and it would end at 9:00. I was excited but a little nervous too. I could probably handle three hours during the dance. What would happen? I was pacing back and forth when my phone started ringing. I looked to see who was calling. Oh no.

"Hey, Adrian …" I said into the phone.

"Hey, Alex. Red mentioned a dance ..."

"Yeah?"

"Um. Are you going to the dance?"

"Yeah. I'm meeting the others at the school. Charlene is going with Josh, and you know Red is going with Nina. Mallory is going with Angel. Oh! Not that way. Not *going with* but going with. You know?"

Oh jeez. I ran my hand down my face, glad that I was not on *FaceTime*.

Adrian chuckled. "You are cute when you are nervous."

"What? Wait ... what?"

"Yeah. Anyway ... I can't really ask you to a dance that's not at my school ..."

"Huh? Do you want to go?" I asked.

"Yes ..."

"Oh, yeah, sure!" I said enthusiastically. "Umm ... okay ... let's go to the dance together."

"Why, Alex," he drawled, using a fake Southern accent. "I thought you would never ask."

I could hear him smirking through the phone. I giggled.

"So ... how are we gonna get there? You want my parents to pick us up or something?" he asked.

"Wait, no ... your parents can't pick us up because they don't know me, and my parents are busy ..." I rambled.

"How were you planning on getting to the dance?"

I tried to remember how to breathe.

"Umm. Gwen was going to ... My sister."

"Can your sister pick me up on the way?" he asked.

"Oh yeah, sure …" I agreed. "But uh …should we like be dropped off at the front or like we take the other entrance or …" I said.

"Whoa. Chill. It's not a big deal," Adrian paused. "Something's a little off with you today. Are you okay?" he asked.

"Yeah. Sure. So, Gwen will pick you up at 5:30. Text me the address, okay? Bye," I said, rushing to get off the phone.

The jelly bean was wearing off.

I was screwed.

.   .   .

I opened the door to the candy shop. The little bell that rang whenever a customer came in did its little chime. I didn't stop to look at the various arrays of handcrafted candies and fine chocolates. I went straight to the counter and saw my jelly bean dealer, whose name I still didn't know.

"So …" he smirked, "how'd it work?"

I didn't reply to his question.

"It's wearing off," I said. "What do I do?"

"Whoa," he said. "Slow down. Tell me how it went."

I sighed. "It's going well. I have new friends, I'm popular, and everything's pretty good. It's everything you said it would be."

He leaned in, "*Everything?*" he asked.

"No. There are other things that aren't great. But those don't matter as much."

"Hmmm." He flashed a wide grin. "Okay, I'm gonna give you one last thing," he said.

He held out another tin. This one was lavishly decorated with gold and jewels of all colors.

"That's the permanent one," he said. "You won't see me again. After you take this, you will know the right thing to say. The right thing to do. You'll know how to make people like you. And having people like you will become important."

I looked at him for a second as he continued.

"Popular people drive this world, Alex. They always have. How do you think the people in charge became in charge?"

I didn't answer, but I got his point.

I paused, looking at the tin in his open hand. I became aware that there was no one else in the candy store on a Saturday morning. There was no other sound. The smell of sugar, normally so soothing, had become suffocating. My eyes flitted between him and the tin. I looked around and saw that the chalkboard, usually displaying the candy of the week, was filled with complex math equations.

"Why do you have math equations on the board?" I asked cautiously.

"Can you figure it out?" he smirked, his brown eyes glinting in the light.

I looked at the algebra equation and realized, no. I didn't know the answer. The numbers just swirled in front of me, not making sense.

His grin widened. "Someone else will wish to be a math genius. I have to get that gift from someone," he drawled.

My mouth went slack. I looked between him and the tin, still in his outstretched hand.

"Who are you?" I asked.

He smiled slyly, taking a small bow. "Finlay Atrion, at your service."

I started to pull my hand back.

He continued, "How did your morning conversation go with Adrian? Is he still enamored by your stunning conversation?"

"*What* are you?" I asked, firmer this time.

His golden eyes looked a little more snakelike as his lips pressed into a thin line.

"I'm an Atrion, Alex." he said. "We fix things—broken things."

"I'm not broken!" I said.

"Are you sure Alex?" he smiled. "Isn't everyone a little broken?"

I snatched the tin out of his hand before I could think, desperate to leave.

"Thanks," I said, heading for the door.

"Wait!" he said. I stopped. "One more thing."

"What?" I asked.

"You don't have to pay for it," he said, the suffocating smell dissipating. "You already did."

. . .

I rushed out of the candy shop. The dance would be soon. But the feelings. What he said. I ran to my room. I didn't have a lot of time for emotions, though. No time for questions. Everything would be okay soon.

I slipped on my blue dress. It looked like I was wearing a flowing river of pure beauty. I twirled around and realized I felt beautiful. I started doing the finishing touches on my makeup, trying to distract myself from everything. I'll be okay, I told myself. I walked into Gwen's room to let her know I was ready.

When I walked in, she stared. A little smile formed on her lips.

"You look gorgeous," she said.

"Thanks," I said.

We were silent for a little bit, and then I spotted something. It was the same tin I got when I had my first jelly bean.

But it looked different. Instead of the red and black gems, it had blue and green gems.

I blinked once. Twice.

"Did you …?" I asked.

"Yeah. I thought you'd notice that," she said.

"But you're not awkward," I said.

"Yeah. But I didn't like being responsible. I went to a candy shop one day and complained that I just wanted to have some fun. The shopkeeper gave it to me, and I ate it. It ruined a ton of things." She looked up, seeming to remember something. "But I learned how to be better."

I was dumbfounded.

It was silent for a minute.

"Everyone has something they are struggling with, Alex."

I turned to leave, but I stopped myself.

"Hey. Thanks," I said.

Gwen smiled wistfully. "Let's get going so you can have the time of your life."

.　　.　　.

The cafeteria had been transformed. All the tables were moved to the back. The theme of the dance was Hollywood, so there was a red carpet as we entered, just like when celebrities stepped out of their limo. A black and gold balloon arch stood above the entrance. Gold stars were hanging on the wall, and people were signing them as if they were in the hall of fame.

"Whoa! Look at that décor!" I said.

"Yeah. It's pretty awesome," Adrian replied.

He wore a white collared shirt and a gray vest with black slacks.

When we walked in the door, I handed Ms. Esma a small index card with our names on it.

She smiled and said softly to me, "Nice to see you, Alex. Have a good evening."

"Here is *Alex Heldisch* and *Adrian Ellisberg!*" my Civics teacher boomed when we entered.

I smiled at Adrian, and he smiled back. A DJ was playing loud music, and the dance area was still mostly empty. He took my hand, and we walked toward the food stands. The food stands weren't in the lunch line; there were actually little stands decorated like food trucks that displayed the many arrays of steaming hot dogs, burgers, and pizza. I picked out a kosher hot dog and grabbed coke from a soda stand. Adrian wasn't really a sugar person, but even he got a root beer for himself.

I looked at the pizza stand and read what it said at the top.

"*Mystic Pizza?*" Adrian read.

The person working at the pizza stand looked up from what she was doing. "Yeah, this is what happens when parents decorate with no oversight. Want pepperoni?"

"Nah. I'm Jewish," I said.

The person from behind the stand stared at me blankly.

Adrian spoke up, "No pig for her." He turned to me. "Do you mind if I get pepperoni?"

I shook my head.

"One cheese slice and one pepperoni slice, please," he said.

The girl rolled her eyes and went to get the pizza.

That was the moment *The Pops* strode into the room like they owned the place, complete in their dresses and accessories, catching the eye of the crowd.

Charlene was a stunning sight in her rose dress. The bottom was a light gray with some sort of sheen to it. Her espresso-colored hair was extra curly, and she looked radiant. Ava and Mallory followed behind her in their dresses. Ava's was a vibrant purple, and Mallory's a seafoam green. Nina was across the room with Red, wearing a shimmering gold dress that complemented the gold beads in her black hair, completing the look overall. They all saw me and rushed over, complimenting me on my dress and makeup. Then they noticed Adrian.

"Ooooh," they squealed.

I felt my face become flushed. Adrian put his arm around my waist. This made my blush creep into my neck, but I was enjoying the positive attention.

"Ummm … Alex? We need to talk," Charlene said.

"Hey … I'm gonna go catch up with Red. Plus, I want to try a gyro from the Greek Wedding food stand," Adrian said.

"Yeah, sure." And then I said, "See if they have Shawarma!"

Josh and Red took the cue and headed off to try some food.

"What?" I asked after the boys left.

"I think it's time we fixed a mistake," Mallory said.

I was confused at first, but Mallory took my hand and led me over to my old friends. We walked over to Thomas and the rest of my old group.

They all stood rooted to their spots, watching us approach. Perry leaned in closer to Thomas, and he wrapped his hand around her waist. Natalie looked down, not making eye contact with me. I saw Angel look at Ava, who gave her a small nod.

Charlene stood in the front with the rest of us behind her in a V shape.

She said with authority, "You need to stop ignoring Alex. She didn't do anything wrong."

Thomas scoffed. "She told me she hated me. In front of the entire gym class. That seems like something she did wrong."

I tried to walk away, but Mallory just squeezed my hand tighter.

"Stop," Charlene said, exhaling. "*She* didn't do anything wrong. *We* did it."

Thomas' eyebrows knitted together, not understanding.

Charlene continued, "We dared her to say she hated you, but she refused. She stood up to all of us rather than say anything bad about you. That was the second time she had stood up to me. I didn't like that. So, we edited her voice, so it seemed like she said she hated you. It was immature and mean." She turned to look at me. "I'm really sorry, Alex."

The other *Pops* nodded, quietly saying they were sorry.

My throat started to feel tight, and I began blinking so I would not cry. I didn't realize how badly I needed an apology until just now.

Charlene turned to face my old friends. Her body language changed and became challenging, more what I was accustomed to seeing.

"Actually," she said dramatically, "the idea to destroy her friendship with Thomas and embarrass him was Perry's. She wanted Alex out of the way, so you would ask her to the dance."

Thomas pulled away from Perry.

Thomas looked at her. "What did you do?"

Perry looked back and forth between Thomas and Charlene, who folded her arms over her chest.

Brit said, "I don't see what the big deal was. It was just a joke."

"Shut up, Brit!" Perry snapped.

Natalie burst in, "A joke?"

Thomas shook his head in disbelief. "What did you do, Perry?"

Nina moved closer to me. "I wish I had popcorn right now. This is so worth the calories."

Perry turned to Thomas and began fumbling to explain, "Alex was always monopolizing you! All you did was talk about her and your stupid fandoms. Every time we would flirt, she would burst in and say something random."

"That's how she is. She didn't do that to get in the way!" he yelled back.

Huh? They flirted? When did that happen?

Perry rolled her eyes, "Oh, please. No one could miss that. She did that on purpose."

Mallory whispered to me, "Did you do that on purpose?"

I leaned into her ear, still keeping my eyes on the fight. "Nope. I'm usually pretty clueless."

Charlene joined in, "I might agree. She did wear that Halloween-colored outfit last week."

I laughed.

Perry turned towards me, thinking I was laughing at her. "I'm so sick of you. You get everything you want. You had Thomas, and then you somehow got to be super popular. Whatever. I'm done." Perry stomped off, Brit following her.

My eyes were wide, trying to emotionally catch up.

Thomas walked up to me. *The Pops* stepped in close to me protectively.

What a difference a week makes.

"Thomas …" I said, taking a step towards him.

He rubbed the back of his neck with his hand. "Alex, I … really misunderstood what happened. I was mad at you because it sounded like you didn't want to be my friend. And also because I thought you said that you didn't like me in front of the whole gym class. I should have talked to you, but then I saw you hanging with … *The Pops* … and I just assumed the worst."

Angel and Natalie stepped forward.

"We are so sorry, Alex," Angel said.

Natalie nodded.

"So … are we good?" Thomas asked.

"Well, not all the way, but yeah. I think we are," I said.

Adrian walked over to me. "Hey … no shawarma. But I did get you hummus with pita." He turned to the rest of the group and said, "Hi, nice to meet you. I'm Adrian, Alex's boyfriend."

Everyone was silent for a minute.

My eyebrows shot up. I have a boyfriend?

Natalie and Angel yelled in sync, "You have a *boyfriend*? SQUEEEEEEEEEEEEEE!"

Thomas raised his eyebrows in a playful way that read, "Boyfriend?"

Mallory laughed and suggested, "Hey, let's take photos!"

•   •   •

"This one is the best," Adrian said, showing me the one Mallory had posted.

I leaned into him, looking at the photo. "I like that group one. But I really like the one Nina snapped of you and me."

I pulled up the one with us dancing, not looking at the camera.

"We're here," Gwen said, looking in the rearview mirror.

Adrian and I got out of the backseat. His home was a small, charming-looking house. He held my hand, walking to his front stoop.

When we got to the doorstep, he said, "You looked beautiful tonight." He brushed the back of his hand along my cheek.

"Thanks," I blushed.

"This was the best night ever," he said.

"It was only because of you," I replied.

I looked into his light brown eyes as he looked into mine. He leaned in for a hug and held me there for a long time.

"Bye!" I said.

"Bye, Alex!" he said, smiling radiantly.

I walked back to the car, almost stumbling as I looked over my shoulder to wave goodbye again.

As I pulled myself into the passenger seat, Gwen asked, "Not ready for a kiss yet?"

"Har har," I said sarcastically.

"Alright," she said, smirking.

"Gwen …" I complained.

"Fine," she said.

I saw the candy store come into view.

"Wait!" I said suddenly. "I need to make a stop."

Her eyebrows knitted, but she didn't say anything. She pulled the car up to the shop, looking at me anxiously. I got out of the car and walked into the shop.

Finlay was sitting at the counter, tinkering with something again. I placed the jelly bean container on the counter, and he stood up.

"Didn't want it?" he asked, looking at it for a split second.

"Some things aren't worth the cost," I replied.

We stood staring at each other for a long time. My brown eyes to his golden-red. Finlay smirked before taking the container off the counter. "See you around, Alex," he said.

"No, I don't think so," I replied.

I walked to the car but turned to take one last glance at the shop.

What was once a bright shop bustling with life was now entirely empty, the lights turned off, and the furniture cleared. I blinked and looked again.

Empty.

I opened the car door and got in.

"Gwen, the store's cleared out," I said, turning to her.

"What do you mean?"

"It's all empty, the furniture's gone, there's dust everywhere and—"

"Okay, I think we need to fix your sleep schedule," Gwen said.

She looked over at me with a wide toothy grin.

"What?" I asked.

"Nothing. I'm just happy I get to keep putting up with my awkward little sister."

"Me too, Gwen. Me too."

She put the car into drive, and I let the candy shop disappear in the rearview mirror.

"**B**arukh ata Adonai muhkadash Shabbat."

There was a moment of silence as the note left my mouth, quieting the room.

I ducked behind the stand as everyone launched candy gems through the air.

The crowd erupted as children began racing to grab the candy, but much to their dismay, I had gotten a giant handful. After my fair share of Bat and Bar Mitzvahs, I knew the importance of getting more candy than everyone else. Not because it actually mattered. But because the candy was delicious.

Rabbi Kamensky burst out, saying, "We wish you a sweet transition into adulthood!"

I stood up, putting my winnings on the edge of the bimah. I straightened my yarmulke, adjusting the folds of my dress. It was a flowing powder blue dress with a corset in the back, with gold and white flowers blooming across its silky layers.

The crowd was louder than it had been during the entire service, but the chatter gradually quieted as the rabbi stepped up to the bimah. As he walked up, he adjusted his black-rimmed glasses. It was finally time to give my Bat Mitzvah speech.

"Shabbat Shalom," he said, his voice booming across the room. The congregation responded with the same words as he continued, "Today, we are celebrating Alexandra Heldisch as she becomes a woman on this occasion."

I cringed slightly at the sound of my first name. I still hated *Alexandra* with a passion, but I was willing to put up with it for five more minutes. Popularity couldn't change everything.

I beamed a little as he continued, praising my hard work over the past three years.

After a while of talking, he said, "Now, Alexandra has prepared a speech about her Torah portion that she would like to share with all of you."

He stepped down from the bimah as I stepped up.

"Shabbat Shalom," I said into the microphone. "Yitro, my Torah portion, talks about the Ten Commandments, but there's more to the story than simply the rulebook of Judaism. It's about Yitro, a seemingly normal person that truly changed the course of the religion."

I continued, "To begin, Yitro was Moses's father-in-law and was a priest of another religion. He first showed up by bringing Moses's wife, Zipporah, and his kids back. He then admitted that Moses's G-d is powerful and gives an offering. Yitro recognized their differences and decided not to convert, but he did acknowledge Moses's G-d respectfully."

"Let's back up for a minute. Yitro is one of the only Torah portions named after a person. Moses doesn't have one named after him. Neither does Abraham, Issac, Jacob, Sarah, Rebekah, Rachel, or Leah. But Yitro does have one named after him." I went on, "This highlights that people who are different from us, like Yitro, can be important, and we can learn from each other. Diversity is critical to society's growth. It's not just about differences; it's about accepting people's uniqueness. And my generation has the privilege of experiencing diversity to its fullest."

I looked across the crowd at my friends. Angel was leaning on Ava's shoulder, their hands intertwined, both smiling softly. I saw Nina stealing some of Thomas's candy while he wasn't looking. She winked at me as she popped a red candy gem into her mouth. Natalie grinned and gave me a thumbs-up sign.

"For instance, I appreciate that my friends have come to support me, even though three hours of Hebrew probably sounds like gibberish to them. And I'm also thankful for those who are Jewish who came out to support me as well. As I look out, I see all the diversity, and I am thankful for you all."

So much had changed over the past few months, and thankfully, most of my friends hadn't. There were still a few exceptions, though. Mallory didn't show; I told her parents about her depression and cutting, and she flipped out on me. Over the past month, she did seem to get happier. There were times I would see her in the hallway, and I swore she was going to come over to talk to me. But she never did. One day, maybe she will. And without my social signaling jelly bean, I was too weird for Charlene, so she dropped me as well. It still hurt to know that she was no longer my friend.

"But to continue, there's an even deeper meaning in the passage. There's something missing in the text. And what is missing is just as important as what's there.

"The omission here is Moses's lack of affection towards his family when Yitro brings them to him. He hadn't seen his family in *years*, and he treats his family as he would treat a stranger. How would Zipporah and his kids feel? Moses was so focused on his work, so overwhelmed with creating this society, that he forgot to show love to his family and openly appreciate them."

I took a deep breath, saying another line, "A few months ago, I began to realize what I was missing. I was missing friends—actual friends. I always thought that I wasn't good enough. I was always stressed and panicked. That made me a bad friend. While I felt that they didn't really know me, I hadn't made the effort to know them either.

"But a few months ago, something happened that made things easier. I was able to open myself up and get to know people. I was able to see what they were struggling with. And because of all this, some things changed for the better. I found out why I'm so bad at talking; it's because I'm really good at listening."

There were a few scattered chuckles. I made eye contact with Ava, who told her parents she was gay just a few months ago. Ava's parents were confused at first, but they learned to accept her sexuality. Nina told her mom she didn't want to be a model, but she never told anyone else about her prior food-related secret.

"Now I know that it's the inside that counts. And that some things aren't worth the cost." I looked at Gwen and winked.

I breathed in and continued, "I chose the Trevor Project for my Bat Mitzvah fundraiser because for LGBTQ kids, true and honest support for them is what is missing. The Trevor Project provides hotlines for LGBTQ teens who are struggling. Not everyone has family and friends who support them and truly *see* them. Yitro connected with Moses and told him his religion was valid, even though he wasn't Jewish. The Trevor Project seeks to do the same exact thing with LGBTQ teens; to show that their sexual orientation and gender identity is valid even though their friends and family may be different.

"And, like how Moses needed Yitro's help, I couldn't do this by myself either. I would like to thank Rabbi Kamensky and Naomi Strict for teaching me everything I needed to know for this day and supporting me through these long three years. I would also like to thank my parents, Debra Goldman and David Heldisch, as well as my sister Gwen for all being there for me and helping me get to this day. You all are amazing. Lastly, I would like to thank my friends and family who came to see me and support me today. I greatly appreciate your support."

I clapped my hands. "Okay, everyone! One more song, and we can eat," I said after I finished.

Everyone laughed and began to sing Adon Olam. There were cheers as I stepped off the bimah. After my family hugged me and Rabbi Kamensky shook my hand, Adrian was waiting to congratulate me.

He leaned in and gave me a kiss on the cheek. "That was amazing," he said, his eyes shining brightly.

Raaj ran up to me. "I'm so sorry to interrupt, but Jay and I have to get to the math competition. I wish we could stay for the lunch."

"Of course. I'm so happy you were able to make it!" I said, giving him a quick hug.

Adrian stood off to the side, awkwardly putting his hands in his pockets.

"We'll see you tomorrow for practice. Remember, you have to fill in for me next weekend because I'm out of town!" Raaj yelled, trying to weave his way through the crowd of people.

"I can't wait. See you tomorrow!" I waved to Raaj until his brightly patterned tie was covered up by everyone else.

Adrian turned to me. "You know I'm competing in next week's tournament, right?"

I grinned and said, "Well, I know you're a mature man and won't mind losing to his girlfriend."

Adrian failed to stifle his laughter and pulled me in tight. "Nope, I won't mind one bit."

.　　.　　.

"I gotta be honest with you guys," I said. "I'm way less awkward in Hebrew than I am in English," I said as I sat down at the designated teen table.

Thomas took a bite of a bagel and asked, "Okay. Explain some of these things to me again. Why are we all wearing these discs on our heads?

Nina shoved her elbow into them. "They are pronounced *yah-muh-kuh*," she said, emphasizing each syllable. "Just call it a kippah. Honestly, you grew up with her. How have I passed you in my knowledge?"

Nina leaned over and grabbed a chip with hummus from Thomas' plate.

"Hey, get your own hummus," Thomas said.

Nina laughed, "I already ate mine. You need to share."

I glanced over at Angel and raised my eyebrows. She nodded, and my eyes went wide. Wow, Thomas and Nina. I did not see that coming. I knew Nina and Red broke up after some time since Nina realized it was an unhealthy relationship, but I still didn't expect it.

Adrian stood up, "I need to get some cake that has my girlfriend's face on it. Anyone want anything?"

"Oh! Get me some of her hair," Natalie said.

I groaned while the others laughed.

"What? I like the chocolate frosting," she explained.

"Umm ... can you get me something without my face? I'll be right back." I excused myself and walked to the bathroom.

I went inside one of the stalls and pulled out my phone. Electronics weren't allowed during Shabbat, but I felt a buzz in my pocket.

My phone came on, and a text popped up.

Charlene:
I'm sorry I missed it. I know it was a big deal. Talk to you on Monday.

Me:
K. Thanks. Bye

I shut off my phone, unsure about my feelings.

I inhaled, adjusting the tallit and yarmulke before I went back out to my friends. My real friends, who laughed when I made mistakes and when I interrupted them. Friends who appreciated me when I could listen and keep things private and who told me it was okay even when I kept apologizing. I leaned into the mirror and looked at the reflection.

So. Am I weird?

Yes. Yes, I am.

But this time, it was *my* choice.

ACKNOWLEDGMENTS

This book has been quite the ride throughout the years. As a fifth grader, it was just a dream of a book, but my friends and family did so much to make this work possible. Thank you to my mother, Jennifer, for inspiring me and giving me so much helpful advice to continue this journey. I would also like to thank my father, Chris, for reading the work and supporting me.

I would also like to thank my first instructor, Jackson Pearce, who guided me in writing this novel. It was so fulfilling to have you support me and help me finally get this story on paper. I can never thank you enough for pushing me to accomplish this. I would also like to thank my editor Melissa Savage for mentoring me in the Young Inklings program to finally achieve this dream. You're a fantastic person and an even better editor. It was such a pleasure to work with you every week to make this novel the best it could be.

So much of my gratitude goes toward who this book is dedicated to, my best friend and sister, Veronica. When I began writing this book three years ago, she offered me so much insight and advice on how to write my characters, and always stuck with me throughout. I couldn't have asked for a better sister and writing partner. She was my greatest support through this novel and inspired me and motivated me so much. Not to mention she designed the fantastic cover for this book, which I'm incredibly grateful for. Veronica, if you're reading this, I want you to know that you are the best person I've ever met, and you've always been there for me. That's more than anything I could've wished for.

Thank you to Lauren for providing lengthy edit suggestions for my work as well as my parents, who read my book and worked with me on it.

The rest of my thanks goes to my friends who helped beta read. Melia, Kirra, Dinah, Annah, and Evey, I thank all of you for being patient and supporting me throughout this process.

I couldn't have done this without you all. Thank you so much for making this possible.

ABOUT THE AUTHOR

Rebekah Brown (she/her) is a newly seasoned writer in the eighth grade. She attends a technology program in Florida and plays the trombone in the symphonic band. She enjoys spending time with her friends and creating stories with them. Her other interests include drawing, writing fantasy, watching movies with her family, swimming on her local team, and fencing. This is her first book, and she plans to continue her writing journey for years to come.

And unlike her main character, math is her least favorite subject.

·   ·   ·

You can follow Alex's journey on *Instagram* @alex_sociallyawkward.

You can find Alex's *Spotify* Playlist by searching for MoonRose15.

AUTHOR'S NOTE

When I first came up with the idea for *Hi, I'm Socially Awkward,* I was in fifth grade. I had a hard time navigating socially around that time, and I felt self-conscious and anxious often. Writing and drawing was my own way to escape from the world, and I had always held it close. Like many other friends I had, I despised the *popular girls* and continued despising them until, after a camping trip, and got to know a few of them. And after that, the idea formed itself. A girl that was awkward like myself, who got a chance to be popular. So many things have changed since I started writing, and it was one heck of a journey. This book followed me through friend group changes, new phases, fandoms, sometimes even rewriting entire characters from scratch. But throughout every edit I made, I always wanted to share this story because it always felt so close to me. So, no matter if you're awkward or popular, you have to know that everyone is struggling with something. You just don't know what that is yet.

All profits from this book will go to The Trevor Project. The Trevor Project is an American nonprofit organization that focuses on suicide prevention for lesbian, gay, bisexual, transgender, queer, and questioning youth. They offer a toll-free telephone number where confidential assistance is provided by trained counselors. You can donate directly to this organization at www. thetrevorproject.org

BONUS CONTENT

MONDAY

"This just feels really stupid. Can't we talk to her?" Angel asked.

Perry rolled her eyes. "We've been over this. She has to understand what she did. It's only been a weekend."

Thomas looked down, kicking a small pebble.

"I know she said she hated me. But that doesn't seem right." He looked over to Angel. "I mean, we've known her forever. You know how she is. She must've tripped over her words."

"I know," Angel said. "You're probably right; I mean, can we really trust Charlene and those people?"

"Well, it was a recording," Natalie said. "It seemed legit. But you still have a point."

"This is ridiculous," Perry said. "I saw that myself. She's just trying to hurt you."

"Shut up, Perry!" Angel yelled.

The group went quiet. Angel never yelled.

"We've been friends with Alex for eight years," she said coldly. "I know you're new, but you don't know her like we do, so just stop it!"

Perry had turned red but didn't open her mouth again.

"I want to talk to her," Thomas sighed. "I need to figure out why this all happened. We all know it was probably a misunderstanding."

"But I was there," Brit said firmly. "She definitely meant it."

"I didn't ask you," Natalie spat. "If you want to talk to her, go ahead."

"Yeah. I want to see if we can fix this," Thomas said.

Thomas got up from his seat on the bench, walking towards the library. He moved past it as the others followed. Right on time, the bell rang across the campus. He turned to walk to homeroom, sitting down in his seat. The others followed as well, waiting for Alex to arrive.

They looked up and saw Charlene walking into the school, closely followed by Ava, Mallory, Nina … and Alex?

"What the—?" Natalie began.

Thomas's mouth was agape, mirroring the rest of the group. "I don't understand."

"Honestly, I'm so excited for today," Alex commented, pulling herself onto her desk as she pulled out her phone.

She talked with *The Pops* and said some things none of them could hear, but they seemed to be getting along. Nina went over to Alex's side, and they both took a selfie.

All of them felt the *Instagram* notification ding from their phones.

Perry looked furious. "I know what happened," she snapped. "Alex must've done the dare to get into their group. She decided that being popular was more important than your friendship."

Angel shook her head, "No way! Alex doesn't care about being popular. She wouldn't know what popularity looked like if it walked up and poked her."

Brit spoke up, "Did you see her clothes? Those are new."

"Yeah, she even *looks* like one of them. I bet she planned this. You all really think she just suddenly became part of their group? They look way too close for that," Perry added.

Thomas's neck started to turn red. "She wants to be friends with them?"

Angel had her phone out and was texting furiously. "This can't be right."

"Looks like she spent all weekend with them," Brit said as she pulled up *Instagram.*

And there it was—there were at least ten posts with pictures of Alex at the pool, trying on new clothes, and eating burgers with them.

Natalie snatched the phone out of her hand. "I can't believe she would betray us like this."

Perry smirked. "Yeah. She betrayed you." She shared a side-long glance with Brit, who nodded with a smile.

Thomas, Angel, and Natalie stood together, staring after Alex, who walked away with her new friends.